THE
UNSPOKEN

THE
UNSPOKEN

THOMAS FAHY

Simon & Schuster Books for Young Readers
New York London Toronto Sydney

SIMON & SCHUSTER BOOKS FOR YOUNG READERS
An imprint of Simon & Schuster Children's Publishing Division
1230 Avenue of the Americas, New York, New York 10020

Book design by Daniel Roode and Karen Hudson
The text for this book is set in Fairfield.
Manufactured in the United States of America
2 4 6 8 10 9 7 5 3
Library of Congress Cataloging-in-Publication Data
The unspoken / Tom Fahy.—1st ed.
p. cm.
Summary: Six teens are drawn back to the small North Carolina town
where they once lived and, one by one, begin to die of their worst
fears, as prophesied by the cult leader they killed five years earlier,
and who they believe poisoned their parents.
ISBN-13: 978-1-4169-4007-4 (hardcover)
ISBN-10: 1-4169-4007-3 (hardcover)
[1. Cults—Fiction. 2. Murder—Fiction. 3. Dreams—Fiction. 4. Horror
stories.] I. Title.
PZ7.F14317Uns 2008
[Fic]—dc22
2007000850

For my nieces Tommi-Rose and Ellie Lynn,
whose futures are bright indeed.

ACKNOWLEDGMENTS

I am deeply grateful and indebted to Elaine Markson and everyone at the Markson agency for their ongoing support. I also want to extend my sincere thanks to David Gale, his assistant Alexandra Cooper, and the dedicated staff at Simon & Schuster for making this book a reality.

I would have never crossed the finish line without the sagacious feedback of several dear friends—Daniel Kurtzman, Laura Garrett, and Susann Cokal. I can't thank you enough for your generosity and love.

I also extend my heartfelt gratitude to Tom and Eileen Fahy, Mike and Jen, and my enchanting nieces, Tommi-Rose and Ellie Lynn. I am so fortunate to call you family.

CONTENTS

PROLOGUE

Before Jacob Crawley arrived, the town of Meridian, North Carolina, was so small that most folks couldn't tell you where to find it. Even the state map skipped right over it, like it was too much trouble to write down the name, let alone make room for it on a map.

But Jacob changed all that. With an easy smile and a big voice he started to convince people that Meridian was destined for greatness. We just had to be ready for it, he said. We had to open our minds.

One summer afternoon Jacob invited the entire town to the abandoned church on Shady Grove Lane—one of the few streets in Meridian without a single tree on it. Allison once asked her daddy about that name being so out of place, but he was the kind of man who never answered a question directly.

"Some people don't have a good sense for naming things," he told her, and thinking back on Shady Grove Lane, Allison figures he was right.

As she and her daddy squeezed into the old church with the rest of the town, Allison remembers thinking that it was hot as the surface of the sun. Sure, she knew from science class that the sun was so hot that it didn't even have a surface. It was like molten lava all the time. But the heat was something awful that day, and everyone was sweating buckets. Ladies were fanning themselves. Men wiped their brows with the backs of their hands, and little babies started to fuss.

When Jacob finally spoke from behind the podium, his voice seemed to soothe folks. Allison was ten and small for her age, so she could only see bits of him through the crowded pews in front of them. She doesn't remember much of what he said, but the sound of his words . . . now, that she remembers. They buzzed. People started swaying and nodding their heads. Some were even tapping their toes as they listened.

Soon everyone was caught up in the moment, moving their bodies and forgetting about the heat, about the street with no shade outside. That's when Jacob announced he was a prophet—a new prophet for a new age. Well, as you can imagine, those words stopped everything, kind of like the time Tommy Doyle belched in front of Baby Jesus during the Nativity scene at the school Christmas pageant—no one knew whether to laugh or to be real angry. So the church got quiet, and everyone waited for Jacob to say something else. To explain himself. Instead he left the pulpit, walked up the aisle to Allison's pew, and touched her daddy on the shoulder.

Jacob bowed his head slightly, and all she could see was his silver white hair. He was still for so long that Allison wondered if he'd fallen asleep. She had never known anyone who could sleep while standing up. Well, cows could, but not people. So she figured Jacob must have been concentrating real hard. Her daddy just got that strange half smile on his face—the same one he got after asking her for the "umpteenth time" to clean up her room. ("Umpteenth" was his word for a number that was too high for counting. Her daddy was a patient man, but that smile meant he was just about fed up.)

"Sometimes," Jacob began, lifting his head and looking at her daddy with those yellow eyes, "sometimes, we carry so much pain inside that we can hardly breathe. It's like our hearts just collapse. . . . That's what happened on the night you lost your daughter, isn't it? On the night she was taken from you."

Allison's daddy didn't move. It was as if someone had slapped him in the face and he was too shocked to respond.

"I can help you breathe again," Jacob continued. "It's not too late."

Without waiting for a response, Jacob lifted his hand from her daddy's shoulder and moved farther down the aisle toward old Mrs. Haggerty. By then Allison wasn't paying attention anymore. She just looked at her daddy, who stood there with his mouth hanging open and his eyes blinking.

How could Jacob know about Melanie? Allison wondered. She was killed almost two years ago, and no one in town talked about it. Sure, everyone knew, but knowing and saying are two different things. It was possible Jacob had seen it in the news, Allison considered. The local paper had run a story about it, but Allison couldn't read it all the way through. To her, that night seemed too private . . . too painful for strangers.

After Jacob's first time at the pulpit Allison and her daddy started going to his weekly gatherings at the abandoned church. They weren't the only ones, either. Dozens of folks filled the church every week, listening to Jacob's ideas about our troubled times, about the fear infecting this country, about the end time and the new world that would come. Allison assumed it was powerful stuff because all of the grown-ups started to think Jacob was right. But she couldn't stop thinking about Shady Grove Lane and how it sounded like the name for a cemetery.

A few months later Jacob invited all of them to live in several cabins outside of town, not far from the old church. That was the day Jacob decided on a name for his ministry—the Divine Path. And that's what they started calling themselves.

The Divine Path.

That was two years ago, and in the last two years Allison has thought about that story too many times for counting. Once a week Jacob insisted that everyone share a "moment of enlightenment" with the other believers. Allison wasn't exactly sure what that meant, but she always told this story because that day in the church was the first time since Melanie's murder that her father seemed to have hope. It was the first time he seemed like her daddy again.

Now—with the fire raging behind her and Ike Dempsey gripping her hand so tight that she can't feel her fingertips— it's the only story she can think about. The heat from the blaze starts to make her back sweaty, and she leans forward. Standing in a circle with the only friends she has ever known, she looks around at the six of them, heads bowed as if they are too ashamed to look at one another.

We did it, she thinks. *All of us.*

Except it was her idea. She was the first one to say it out loud: "We have to kill Jacob. We have to destroy this place."

They were too late to save their parents, though. Jacob must have poisoned everyone else hours before the blaze started. Moments later angry winds carried the flames to the main hall, and it caught fire like dried autumn leaves. There is nothing they can do to stop it from burning, but they can't watch, either. It's just too painful to see your whole life—your family, your home . . . everything you thought you cared about—disappear in an instant. So they stand in a circle, facing one another instead, and listen to the sounds of the crackling flames.

What scares Allison most is the idea that Jacob somehow knew what was going to happen. That he knew the six of them would do this. Hadn't he told everyone that the Divine Path would be devoured in a wall of flame? That someone would betray him just as Judas betrayed Christ?

He made other predictions too. He foresaw terrible things happening to them—visions of their worst fears coming true.

"In five years' time," Jacob told each of them privately, "your greatest fear will consume you. It will rob you of your last breath."

Listening to the fire sizzle and gasp behind her, Allison wonders if he wasn't just trying to scare them.

"What if it comes true?" she asks to break the silence, her voice hoarse and unsteady.

But no one looks up or says a word. They just hold hands as the air around them fills with smoke and the white ash of burning flesh. . . .

Five years later . . .

1
DREAMCATCHER

The bright red blood on Allison's pillow reminds her of "Snow White"—not the watered-down Disney version with magic kisses, dwarfs named Dopey, and singing animals. The older story with a hateful queen who wants to eat a young girl's lung and liver. The one that ends when the queen is tortured to death in red-hot iron slippers.

Now, that's a good story, Allison thinks with a sly smile. Better than the image that woke her—a boy being swallowed by black green waters. Mouth open. Bubbles where a scream would be.

As she sits up, the sickly-sweet taste of blood fills her mouth, and she can feel the bumpy surface of her tongue. She must have bitten it in her sleep, she realizes. Her eyes are stinging bad, and her forehead pounds like the drum set that her pimply foster brother plays in the garage every afternoon.

She looks back at the red stain on the pillow, trying to remember if she took her medication yesterday. She has some kind of seizure every few weeks now. They're so common that they don't faze her much anymore. Sometimes she's surprised how much a person can get used to. How much pain and fear and heartbreak.

But that dream was different. She hasn't had one like that for years.

Since right before the fire.

Of course, she probably wouldn't be sick anymore if Jacob

hadn't taken away her pills back then. He thought the medication would interfere with her dreams, so he kept it from her.

"Dying might interfere with them too," she always wanted to say, but Allison was too afraid of Jacob for that. Jacob had ways of punishing that stayed with you.

Mostly, Jacob thought the seizures made her dreams more vivid, more prophetic—a word he used lots to explain away the things that folks didn't like about the Divine Path. Allison could never remember anything after a seizure anyway, but sometimes when she came to, an image would flash before her eyes, like the way a lightbulb flares up before it burns out forever. That's what happened when she was first diagnosed with epilepsy—seven days before her sister's murder. She was sitting at the kitchen table, flicking milky Cheerios at Mel's face, when her body went cold and hard.

Later, Daddy told her how she suddenly fell to the floor and let out a cry. "Like someone was squeezing the air right out of you," he said. "Then you started shaking something fierce."

Allison doesn't remember any of those things. But she does remember Doc Hillerman coming over to see her. That made her nervous. Doctors never come to your house—even in a small town where the nearest hospital is thirty miles away. Besides, she didn't want anyone around, let alone Doc Hillerman, who always smelled like olives, but it wasn't up for discussion, Ma said.

Doc Hillerman got there quick, and he didn't waste any time chitchatting, either. He walked right over to Daddy's leather chair in the living room, where Allison was sitting, and he asked her how she was doing. That made her nervous too because Doc Hillerman usually liked to play around first—pretending that he couldn't remember her name or giving her candy for medicine. But instead of trying to make her laugh, he took out his stethoscope and leaned in close to listen to her heart. She could smell the olives on his body, and it made her stomach turn. Then he flashed a little white light in her eyes.

That's when it happened. In an instant she saw a picture of her sister lying in bed, black blood covering her throat like a scarf.

Allison screamed so loud that Doc Hillerman dropped his penlight.

She didn't care, though. She was convinced that something terrible had happened to Melanie. Struggling to get off the soft cushions that seemed to be swallowing her, Allison blurted out her sister's name—"Mel!"

"Where's . . . ," she started to say, still trying to push herself away from the chair, but before she could finish, her sister came running into the room with Ma.

She was just fine . . . for seven more days.

"Allison," her foster mother calls up the stairs. "You're going to be late for school. Hurry up."

The voice startles her, as if someone has just shaken her awake, and Allison looks at the clock on her bedside table: 7:14.

"Crap," she mutters. Math class is first period, and her precalculus teacher, Mrs. Jenkins, has the patience of a rabid pit bull. Allison won't just get detention for being tardy. That would be too easy. She is going to get another lecture on personal responsibility and God knows what else. "There are two types of people in the world, Miss Burke"—Mrs. Jenkins always begins the same way, her narrow glasses perched at the tip of her nose and a silver pendant of the Virgin Mother dangling between her freckled breasts—"those who show up and those who don't. . . ."

Blah, blah, blah, Allison thinks as she gets out of bed and stumbles toward the bathroom. Her tongue throbs, and her head is still spinning from the seizure and from the memories of her sister. She needs her medication. She needs to *not* be thinking about Mel right now. Sometimes it feels like too much, Allison admits to herself. Melanie and Daddy. Ma. Jacob and the terrible things that happened back then. All of these memories feel like a weight that's too heavy for one person to carry.

In the bathroom the cold tile floor stings Allison's feet as she stands in front of the medicine cabinet and grabs the pills from the top shelf. Standing here, she also looks at her reflection in the mirror—the brown, shoulder-length hair, the green eyes, and, of course, a new spot of acne above her upper lip.

"Double crap," she says, before popping the pill into her mouth and chasing it with a handful of water from the faucet.

Stepping back into the bedroom, she glances down at her slender body and long white legs. Some of the guys at school stare at her on the days she wears skirts and tight jeans, but they mostly seem to notice the strange mark across her neck. She hasn't gone out without necklaces or scarves in five years. But they don't always cover everything. Sure, she can tell when people at school are whispering about it. But she doesn't care what they think.

Just Bo.

Bo is the boy she has been seeing for about a month now. Six days ago he gave her a silk scarf. He called it a "just-because gift." That's the first time she really let him see her scar. He even ran his fingertips across it that night, while they were making out in the front seat of his father's Mercedes. His touch sent goose bumps down Allison's body.

She wonders what her neck felt like to him. Yeah, she has touched it a thousand times, but your own body never feels the same to someone else. That's what makes being touched so nice. Your flaws disappear, for a while at least, and your body tingles—not just from the feeling, but from knowing that someone else wants to touch you.

"Allison?" her foster mother calls out again.

"Okay," she hollers back. "I'm coming."

Allison doesn't want to say anything about her seizure. She doesn't want to involve her foster parents at all. This illness is part of *her* and her past—the part she wants to control and forget. She can handle it on her own.

In truth, she doesn't really mind her foster parents much. They're nice enough—though they won't win an award for Parents of the Year anytime soon. Like the day Mrs. Packer set fire to the kitchen while trying to kill a cockroach with hair spray. She was screaming and spraying the roach as it scurried across the gas stove, where she was boiling water. Allison isn't sure if Mrs. Packer killed the roach that day, but half the stove and the wall behind it are still black with scorch marks from the flaming hair spray. Or the time Mr. Packer ran the lawn mower over his own foot. He only lost his small left toe, but before going to the emergency room, he insisted on finishing the lawn. "Heck, there was only one more row to cut," he enjoys saying when he retells the story. "And nobody wants to see an unkempt lawn."

"Especially with human toes in it," Allison always wants to add, but she knows better.

Mr. Packer takes lawn maintenance very seriously.

Yeah, they're nice enough, but crazy things happen in the Packer house about once a week. This doesn't bother Allison much. It's kind of entertaining, actually, and most of the time Mr. and Mrs. Packer are too busy managing their own chaotic lives to give much notice to Allison. Which is fine with her. Now, if she could just get eleven-year-old Brutus Packer Jr. to stop practicing the drums . . .

Allison plops down in front of her desk and turns on the computer. Her day doesn't begin until she's checked e-mail. Like coffee or a cold shower, it's the thing that kick-starts every morning.

The connection is molasses slow as usual, but Allison doesn't mind so much today. She feels better sitting down—the dizziness stops, and her head doesn't pound so hard. She looks at the rest of her desk, which is an absolute disaster. Random stacks of CDs. Her cell phone. School textbooks and folders that look like they were just poured out of a bucket. And a can of Diet Coke that's at least five days old.

A dreamcatcher hangs above it all from the desk lamp, and she touches it with her fingers. The circle of yellow and orange cloth reminds Allison of a bright summer day and the orange-haired boy who gave it to her just over five years ago—Ike Dempsey. He had a crush on her, and though Allison liked him, she didn't like him *like that*. She wanted quiet David Holloway, the boy who always lowered his eyes when he smiled, to notice her. She almost kissed David one night in the old tree house—but as Brutus Packer Jr. is fond of saying, "almost" only counts with hand grenades and nuclear war.

The Internet connection finally goes through. Only one message is waiting in her in-box, but she doesn't recognize the e-mail address. The subject line reads: "A Voice From The Past." Allison opens the message and finds a forwarded newspaper article with today's date.

Meridian Herald
Mystery Surrounds the Drowning of a Teenage Boy
by Marcum Shale
The bizarre circumstances surrounding the death of Harold Crawley, a seventeen-year-old boy found in a tobacco field off Route 78, has local authorities baffled.

According to Sheriff Cooper of the Meridian Police Department, an anonymous phone call alerted him to the body two days ago. The cause of death was not immediately apparent, but the county coroner's preliminary findings suggest that Harold Crawley drowned—even though he was found more than thirty miles from the nearest body of water, Lake Haverton.

"Five liters of fluid were found in his lungs," Sheriff Cooper told reporters this morning. "But that doesn't prove anything. This may or may not be a homicide. Right now we have no crime scene and no concrete evidence of foul play."

Sheriff Cooper refused to comment on Harold Crawley's link to the infamous cult the Divine Path, which was founded in Meridian, North Carolina, about seven years ago. Harold was the only son of the cult's leader, Jacob Crawley, and in the summer of 2002 he was one of six children who survived the fire that claimed the lives of Jacob and the other adult members of the Divine Path.

Harold's legal guardian, Ms. Janet Wilton, reported him missing several days ago from their home in Atlanta, Georgia. According to the director of Cicely's Funeral Home, Ms. Wilton has decided to bury Harold in Meridian, where Mr. Crawley purchased a plot for his son a few months before the fire.

A brief memorial service will be held tomorrow at five in the afternoon.

Allison pushes away from her desk with a jolt. Goose bumps run down her spine, and she can feel her stomach dropping away.

"Oh, my God," she mutters.

Allison scans the message again, then studies the user name of the sender: lazarus6. "Lazarus," she says to herself. Like the guy in the Bible that Jesus raised from the dead?

Allison tries to figure out who would send this article. Someone from school? Not likely. She has worked hard to keep her past a secret. When she first moved in with the Packers, her teachers were told that Allison's real parents had died in a car accident, and that story has been around long enough to pass for truth. But if no one from school sent it, who did? Someone from Meridian? Someone who knew about the Divine Path back then? The possibilities make her uneasy. She can tell that the message has been forwarded to several undisclosed recipients. And she wonders if the rest of her old friends have gotten it too. If Ike and David might be reading it right now. If Jade Rowan and Emma Caulder have seen it. If all of them are remembering Jacob's promise.

Allison pictures Harold's face on the night of the fire—his cheeks flushed bright red from the heat. Then she remembers something she hasn't thought of in years. Trees. Harold loved to climb trees. He could scramble up the tallest trunk in the blink of an eye and without ever getting a scratch on his body. Some of the other kids called him Monkey Boy, but that didn't seem to bother him. Allison always thought that he liked being able to get away from time to time. To go where Jacob couldn't find him.

But something is missing from this article. Something that a reporter and the police would never know: Harold couldn't swim. In fact, he was terrified of the water.

A wave of dizziness makes the room shift out of focus, and Allison has to close her eyes to feel steady again. When she opens them, everything is back in focus. She can see the glowing computer screen. The chaotic mess on her desk. The Diet Coke. And the dreamcatcher, which sways slightly from her lamp. She takes it in her hand.

That's what Jacob tried to do—to catch their dreams. Not to keep them safe or to protect them from nightmares. He wanted them to see ugly, horrible things and, more than that, to be afraid. It was fear that fueled his prophecies about the end of the world, about his promise that they would all die from their worst fears.

She wonders if the drowning is just a coincidence, if the thing that Harold was most afraid of killed him. Then Allison recalls the sound of Jacob's voice when he told her that she would die in five years.

"Your greatest fear will consume you. It will rob you of your last breath," he said with a kind of cold pleasure, each word harsh, like metal scraping against cement. The memory makes her shiver.

"Let's get a move on up there," Mrs. Packer says loudly, and Allison looks at the clock again: 7:26.

She is going to be way late for school now, but she doesn't care. She has more important things on her mind. She gets up from the chair slowly, and her entire body feels unsteady and off balance.

What if it's true? Allison asks herself. She glances around her room, unsure of what to do next. She tries to stay calm, to clear her head, but Jacob's promise keeps pressing in around her. She wants to go back to Meridian but is afraid—afraid that Jacob could be right and that all of them are about to die.

But she has to go, she thinks. She needs to see her old friends again. They are the only ones who understand what's about to happen.

2

SCARS

Allison wakes up the next morning with a craving for key lime pie. Sure, she has always had a sweet tooth the size of the Mississippi Delta—which, as any map will tell you, is pretty big—but she usually wants chocolate. Ding Dongs. Double chocolate chip cookies. Hot chocolate. Chocolate chocolate chip ice cream. Chocolate fudge brownies. In a pinch she'll even eat a Hershey's Bar—which, as any chocolate lover will tell you, is second-rate stuff. But recently Allison has been thinking more about key lime pies than chocolate, and she isn't sure why.

Key lime pie was her ma's favorite treat, and she always let Allison and Melanie help with making desserts. "There are two things you need to know about a good key lime pie," her ma would never forget to remind them. "You gotta have *real* key limes from Florida. And you need just the right amount of juice." That last part might sound obvious, but balance is everything. You need enough tartness to make your mouth pucker up and enough sweetness to make you want another mouthful.

And another.

And another.

Balance. Ma, Daddy, Mel, and Allison. Together the four of them were like ingredients. Each one made up an essential part of their family, but when Melanie was gone, nothing tasted right anymore. Ma got real quiet. Daddy stopped laughing. And Allison became invisible, at least to her folks.

Most days when Allison got home from school, her ma would be sitting in front of the television, staring. That may not sound strange at first, but the television was completely broken. You couldn't see anything but your own reflection on the black screen. A few weeks earlier Daddy had plugged one too many things into the same electrical socket, and something inside the TV made a loud popping sound. He liked to joke that Ma's favorite shows were so bad that the TV finally exploded in protest.

But after Mel died, nothing seemed funny anymore. In fact, nothing seemed to work in the Burke house after that—broken towel racks, burned out lightbulbs, leaky faucets. It was as if the entire house was falling apart too.

Three months later her ma wasn't sitting in front of the television, or anywhere else in the house, for that matter. She disappeared on a Saturday afternoon, along with her clothes and jewelry and her favorite cookbook for desserts.

It was the weekend of the state fair, and ma didn't want to go. No amount of persuading would change her mind, either, so Allison and Daddy went without her. It was good to be away, Allison remembers thinking—outside and in the warm sunlight. At the fairgrounds they ate funnel cake and fed the largest pig in the world. They even got tickets for one of those spinning rides whose only purpose is making people dizzy. By the time they got home, Allison's stomach ached from all the spinning and eating—especially the chocolate-dipped Rice Krispies Treats and the rainbow lollipops.

She and Daddy called out when they walked through the door, but no one answered. All the rooms were half empty, and Ma wasn't anywhere to be found. Allison wanted to call the police.

"No," her daddy said, staring at his shoes and speaking in a whisper. "Sometimes people need to disappear for a while . . . she'll come back for you."

Allison figured those words must have hurt a ton—thinking that Ma would return for her daughter but not for her husband. No matter. It turns out he was wrong anyway.

Ma never came back for either one of them.

Before that day Allison had always assumed that disappearing would be hard—that only magicians, CIA agents, and serial killers could do it. But in the Burke house eight years ago Allison learned that disappearing was about as hard as making key lime pie.

And that's not hard at all.

Allison gets out of bed, relieved that there isn't any blood on her pillow. She feels mostly back to normal this morning, though her tongue is sore and swollen, and her head throbs as if Brutus Packer Jr. has been using it for a drum solo. Her duffel bag is ready and sitting by the bedroom door. The gas tank in her car—the ancient car that Mr. Packer gave her when she turned seventeen—is full. And she has left out plenty of crunchy food for John Donne, the Packers' enormously puffy cat.

Now she just needs to get dressed and check e-mail before hitting the road. She hopes Bo has sent his usual good-morning-I'm-thinking-of-you e-mail. For the last month he has written her something every night so she has it first thing. But today her in-box is empty. She's not that surprised, though. Yesterday when Bo asked her why she needed to leave town all of a sudden, Allison couldn't answer.

"It's just something I gotta do," she said.

He got real quiet after that.

How could she tell him—or anyone—about the terrible things that happened back then? About her fear that she might die soon? And if she couldn't explain it to Bo, there was no way Mrs. Packer would understand. So Allison did the only thing she could think of.

"I really need to stay at Heather's place this weekend," she said yesterday after school.

A lie.

"Heather Montgomery?" Mrs. Packer asked, as if Allison knew so many Heathers that it was hard to keep track.

"Yes, Heather Montgomery." *The only Heather I've known my whole life,* she wanted to say. *My only real friend at school.* Instead Allison added, "We have a big history test on Monday."

Another lie.

Allison hates lying. It reminds her of Jacob Crawley and the lies that brought Daddy and her to the Divine Path. The lies that led up to the night of the fire. But Allison doesn't have any other choice right now. She needs to go to Harold's funeral, and there's no way that her foster parents would allow it. As Mrs. Packer would say, "N-period-O-period." So Allison has told two lies. She figures it's better than disappearing like her ma did. She'll never do that to anybody. Ever.

It hurts way too much.

Besides, Heather will cover for her. That's what best friends do. Heather has long blond hair, sky blue eyes, and cheerleader good looks, but she doesn't act like it. She reads books and plays the cello. She's also the only other girl in school who thinks Bill Stringfield, the quarterback of the football team, is the biggest loser in the world. Which he is—and not just because he thinks he's God's gift to women and one time in English class he spelled "potato" with an *e* on the end.

Heather is the only one whom Allison has told about the Divine Path. Well, little bits here and there. But Heather has heard enough to know that Allison has to go back to Meridian. Pronto.

Like Allison, Heather also has a scar, but hers resembles jagged glass and runs from the palm of her hand to the bend in her elbow. She got it in a car accident several years ago when her stepfather-no-more, Tony, drank too many beers at a neighborhood barbecue and insisted on driving Mrs. Montgomery and Heather home. He crashed into an oak tree less than two blocks from their house, giving his wife three broken ribs and cutting up Heather's arm real bad.

And Tony . . . well, he didn't have a scratch on him.

Heather says she doesn't mind the scar so much anymore, but then again, she mostly wears long-sleeved shirts. Allison doesn't mention this. She understands that Heather hates having a permanent reminder of Tony on her body—especially since he left her mother and her about a year after the accident.

Allison knows all about wanting to forget the past.

She knows all about scars, too. . . .

The Confessional was about six and a half minutes from the campsite—far enough away to be out of earshot but close enough to remind you that it was always there. It was the place where Jacob gave penance to those who sinned. At least, that's what Jacob liked to call it—"giving penance."

Allison walked that six and a half minutes enough times to do it blindfolded and backward. She can still picture every step—where the fallen tree blocked most of the stream, where the strange black rocks formed an X on the side of the hill, where you could first see the Confessional under a canopy of thick branches and leaves.

From the outside the Confessional looked like a dilapidated shed with wood as dark as the night sky and walls tilted unnaturally far to one side. It seemed as if a gust of wind could knock the whole thing over. If only. But the inside appeared both bigger and smaller at the same time. Mirrors of different shapes and sizes covered each wall, and even the ceiling was made up of reflective glass. It was like everything was looking back on itself.

A deep, circular pit took up most of the space where the floor should have been. For a long time no one—not Allison or Harold or any of the other kids—got close enough to see inside. They had all sorts of theories about what was there, though. Sharks. Bats. Killer bees. Monsters. Even terrorists.

Once Allison thought she heard a gasping sound like someone choking. Harold heard things too. But he was convinced that something was gurgling, like it was trying to come up for air. No matter. They all had different theories until the day Allison got caught stealing. Until the day she sneaked into Jacob's room to find the box with David's asthma medication.

Jacob's bedroom was more boring than she had expected. A bloodred candle glowed in the far corner, its light flickering across the desktop, and the shelves overflowing with books and yellowing papers. A rectangular rug with faded patterns covered most of the floor, and thick purple drapes hung from the windows. Jacob's bed was against the opposite wall.

Allison hurried across the room to look underneath the bed. The golden box was there—just like Harold had said. She dragged it onto the rug, and its surface held a distorted reflection of everything in the room, like a dirty fun-house mirror. There was no lock or latch on the box. No lid or visible opening. But it wasn't solid wood, either.

Allison tapped on the surface, and she could hear its hollowness. Nothing but four smooth sides. She ran her hands over the entire box again but couldn't figure out how to open it.

It has to be in here, Allison remembers thinking.

Jacob had mentioned the box many times. It was the place where he kept their past—tokens from their lives before the Divine Path, tokens he held on to as if they had some magic power over them. She started to pound the box against the floor, but nothing happened. Not even a dent. She stood up with it in her arms, planning to run outside for a rock or something heavy to smash it open.

That's when Jacob walked through the door.

Her heart stopped beating.

"Good evening, Allison." Jacob smiled, and a slow, easy expression crossed his face. She knew what that meant—another trip to the Confessional.

Less than fifteen minutes later the Doctor brought Allison to the shed. In fact, the Doctor always took "penitent" children to the Confessional. No one had seen him before Jacob moved his followers to the campsite. The Doctor came after that. He just appeared one morning at services, when Jacob brought him up to the podium and introduced him as "the Doctor." Since no one knew what else to call him, the name stuck. He mostly handled basic medical stuff at the camp—bandaging cuts and sprains and that kind of thing. Jacob didn't allow the use of any medicine. He said that God took care of the sick, and that was that.

No one was sure how the Doctor felt about this. He didn't say too much. Besides, his drooping face, unshining black eyes, and grayish skin didn't make you want to strike up a conversation with him. Still, the Doctor always looked worried when someone started coughing or running a fever. He wore that same worried expression every time he escorted Allison to the Confessional. He'd tell her that everything would be fine, that Jacob was doing this for her own good. But she could see that he didn't believe a word of it.

Adults can be the worst liars.

This visit to the Confessional was different from the start. The Doctor walked Allison to the edge of the pit and told her to look inside. She thought it was some kind of trick. Jacob had never said you *couldn't* look inside, but he'd never said it was okay, either. It was as if he just wanted you to wonder, to worry about what was down there. But the Doctor waited . . . waited until she leaned over the uneven edge of the pit and peered down.

Nothing. Empty. *A big black zero,* Allison thought with relief. After all that time she'd spent imagining the terrible things down there, it was only in her head. Either that or the hole was too deep to see anything. She turned back to the Doctor, but he was gone. Instead Jacob stood in the corner of the room, his body reflected in the dozens of mirrors around him.

"What do you want with the box, Allison?"

She didn't answer. In truth, she was sick to death of talking to Jacob.

"I said, what do you want with the box?" Jacob stepped forward, and so did the dozens of Jacobs in the mirrors. His white linen suit and silver hair made his entire body shine.

"I . . ." She hesitated. "Nothing."

Jacob nodded. In an instant he grabbed her shoulders and held her at the ledge.

"Look into the pit again, Allison," Jacob said. "This time I want you to open your eyes. I want you to see what's really down there."

Allison had no choice because Jacob was holding her over the opening now. It wasn't the idea of falling that scared her. It was the realization, maybe for the first time since Daddy and she had become part of the Divine Path, that Jacob would really hurt her. And even worse, that he *wanted* to hurt her. Bad.

"Think about the thing that you're most afraid of, Allison. Concentrate."

Jacob's grip squeezed tighter, and that's when she saw something moving in the darkness below. Allison stared into the pit, trying to see more clearly. The shadows shifted again. Then she could hear a scraping sound, like someone sharpening metal. It got louder and louder, moving closer to the surface. Allison struggled to pull away from the opening, but Jacob held her firmly in place.

"Why do you want to bite the hand that feeds you, Allison?"

Beneath her, something started to glow in the darkness. Red and hot and burning. Then she heard more scratching. Her eyes started to sting and tear. Smoke was suddenly coming up from the pit. It was filling the entire room and scorching the inside of her throat.

"Please," Allison begged. "I can't breathe."

That's when Jacob released her, and Allison fell into the darkness.

"What are you doing?" Brutus Packer Jr. practically shouts across her room, and Allison almost drops the scarf in her hand.

"How many times do I have to tell you to knock, Brutus Packer Jr.?"

He hates the fact that Allison always uses his full name, and his face turns pinkish red. He then glances at the duffel bag by the door and taps it with his foot.

"You're leaving?" his voice cracks somewhat.

Allison suddenly realizes that her neck is not covered, and she wraps the scarf around it, hiding her scar—the scar Jacob put there that day at the Confessional.

"I'm spending the weekend with a friend," she says, and for the first time since she has lived here, Brutus Packer Jr. seems disappointed, almost sad. "I'll be back soon," she adds, and his face brightens briefly.

"Whatever, stinky-pants," Brutus Packer Jr. blurts out before hurrying out of her room.

Allison smiles as she grabs her bag and walks downstairs.

It is still early in the morning, and she can sneak out before Mr. and Mrs. Packer get up. Allison considers waiting around to say good-bye, but she's too anxious for that. It's going to be a long drive, she reminds herself. It's going to be a long trip back to a place she doesn't want to go, to a place that could be dangerous.

She thinks again about Harold and Daddy and Mel and the other kids she used to know. She thinks about key lime pie and how the little things in life make you ache the most for home. And as she starts the engine of her car, she even thinks about Brutus Packer Jr.—her new family, her new life . . . a life she hopes she'll live long enough to come back to.

3

REUNION

Only one road goes into Meridian, and it leads to the town square, which is actually a circle with a thirsty-looking park in the center. If you decide not to stop, the dusty road will loop around and send you right back the way you came. That's how most people think of Meridian—as a town that's more like a revolving door than a place to sit down for a spell.

Not that there is much to stop for. Sure, if you're lucky, you might stumble across the Glory of God Breakfast Barn or the No-Name Tavern, with its maroon pool table and a jukebox that doesn't play music written after 1985. There's even an ice cream parlor at the back of Sutter's Pharmacy. Every summer, on days that were too hot for moving around or thinking, Allison would take Mel there for a root beer float. The red vinyl barstools always felt cool and sticky against your backside, and the icy sodas were almost too big to finish. Almost.

But the truth is that a town with emptiness at its center is like a body without a heart, and Meridian never had much of a pulse—before Jacob, that is.

Allison drives around the town circle, but not too slowly. Small towns have long memories, and someone might recognize her. Most folks would take notice of a car like hers anyway—an off-white 1967 Plymouth Barracuda with a black vinyl top. She looks at the sagging park benches with splintering wood and the mossy green statue of a Confederate soldier. The plaque at his feet is too faded to read, but all of the high school kids used to call him Porn Star because of the way his sword looks when you're standing on either side of him.

Allison turns up Cottonwood Drive and passes by a row of houses that hasn't changed a bit since she left five years ago. On the nearest corner is Mrs. Pinkerton's place, which everyone called Mrs. P.'s Beauty Porch because of the salon at the back of the house. Wiley, her husband, had been the only dentist in Meridian when Allison was a kid, and after he died from a bee sting in the spring of 1998, Mrs. Pinkerton had the two dentist chairs from his office moved to their sunporch. That's when she first started "stylin'," as she liked to call it.

"Those are the nicest things we ever owned, me and Wiley," she always said, pointing to those chairs. "Damn expensive, too."

Mrs. Pinkerton never had a gift for hair, but none of the local women had the heart to say anything . . . or to go anywhere else, for that matter. Needless to say, an appointment at Mrs. P.'s Beauty Porch was risky business. Once you sat in one of those dentist chairs, you never knew how things were going to turn out upstairs, especially if Mrs. Pinkerton started talking about the bee sting. For a long while she swore that Wiley didn't have the brains that God gave a tree frog—*snip, snip, snip*. Otherwise, he wouldn't have been out there in the yard with no shoes on—*snip, snip, snip*.

"Wiley just stepped on the little guy, and the next thing you know, both Wiley and the bee are dead." *Snip, snip, snip.* "Damn waste of a bee."

The shears always snipped more angrily when Mrs. Pinkerton mentioned that bee. Sometimes Allison gripped the arms of that chair so tight that she thought someone would have to pry her off when it was all over. And you could always tell which days Mrs. Pinkerton had gotten to telling that story by the haircuts in town. It wasn't a pretty sight.

A few years later, when Mrs. Pinkerton was less angry about Wiley being gone and she had had time to start missing him something bad, she told folks that he'd been in the garden that day gathering flowers for her.

"Wiley Pinkerton was such a romantic at heart, girls," she'd say with a tear in one eye.

In truth, no one could remember Wiley ever saying or doing anything romantic in his entire life. Other than cleaning teeth and holding the No-Name Tavern's unofficial record for longest belch, Wiley Pinkerton was a regular guy who didn't care much for flowers, love poems, or Hallmark cards.

Allison used to wonder why folks didn't say anything about the new story being so different from the old one, but now—after Mel and Ma and Daddy and the things that happened with Jacob—she understands. It doesn't really matter how Mrs. Pinkerton remembers her husband. Everyone changes the way they see the past at some time or another. It's just something you got to do to make moving on a little bit easier.

As Cottonwood Drive pulls away from town, sycamore trees crowd both sides of the road—thick and green and huddled close together. Allison looks up at the late-afternoon sky. Gray white clouds stretch across the treetops like pulled cotton, and the moisture in the air turns some of the leaves black.

Soon the road seems to give up on the idea of going any- where at all, and it becomes narrow and rough from neglect. If Allison hadn't been here a thousand times before, she'd think she was lost for sure. But right when most people would turn around, the road spills into a clearing that serves as the only cemetery in Meridian.

Marble slabs and stone markers cover the uneven field. Some even date back to the early 1800s, a fact that Allison knows from all her visits to Mel. She and Daddy used to walk past dozens of tombstones before finding her sister's place.

She wasn't far from Lt. James Riley, 1896–1917, and Baby Hawks, who died at three weeks old in 1809.

Sometimes days and even weeks go by before Allison gets that strange feeling in her stomach from missing Mel—like an elevator dropping so fast you almost believe you can fall up. But not a single day passes without some memory of her sister. On the swing that hung from the oak tree in their backyard. At the piano during lessons with Ma. In her room playing with Blue Lizzy, her favorite doll. Or just the mental image of her name carved into that cold black stone:

MELANIE CARMEN BURKE
BELOVED DAUGHTER AND SISTER
1991–1998

Allison has that feeling now as she digs her fingernails into the steering wheel for support. But she knows better. Real pain always sneaks up on you, and there's no bracing for that.

Her stomach starts to settle back down as she pulls into the parking lot of Cicely's Funeral Home—an unremarkable building of worn, almost colorless brick. A handful of cars are parked near the side entrance, including a police car, but otherwise the place is empty.

Allison has been thinking about her friends for most of the drive. She remembers how the six of them were inseparable. How they helped one another get through those years with Jacob, when the world seemed to turn upside down.

It has been strange remembering so much so fast. For five years Allison has been trying to forget, trying to put them out of her mind because she had to. Some memories just hurt too much.

She knows that killing Jacob was the right thing to do, but

there are days when the guilt presses down so hard on her chest that she can't breathe. She took a life. What if that makes her as bad as Jacob somehow? What if that's the reason he killed their parents that day? He could have overheard their plans to burn down the camp. Or maybe he figured it out from studying their dreams. He had said someone would betray him.

Despite the rush of painful memories, Allison is curious about who else may be coming back for the funeral. She has been imagining how each of them received the news of Harold's death. David—the first boy she ever had a crush on—reading the e-mail on a computer at school. Sitting perfectly still and thinking about Jacob's promise. Maybe thinking about her, too. Ike checking it on his phone and feeling the receiver almost slip out of his hand. Emma finding a quiet place—an empty park bench or a library cubicle—and waiting until no one else was around before reading the printout several times. Digesting each word. And Jade skimming it at home—angry enough to tear her computer to shreds.

Allison's legs feel stiff as she gets out of the car. The air is crisp to the point of stinging, and mist dampens her face. She adjusts the maroon scarf around her neck without thinking.

Right now the loose gravel on the ground makes each step feel like Allison is moving through mud. Thick and heavy. She is almost at the side door of the chapel when she hears several low, somber tones behind her.

She turns around.

At the far end of the lot a man wearing a wide-brimmed hat and a black overcoat leans against a car. Only his purplish lips are visible as he presses them against the mouthpiece of a flute. The silver instrument is dull, and it seems too small for his thick, knotted fingers.

Sure, it's possible that Allison didn't notice the rust-colored car at first—old, junky cars don't stand out much to her. Daddy used to work on them in the backyard every weekend. But she is certain no one was standing there before now. One hundred percent certain.

She is still wondering where the man came from when the tune ends and starts all over. This time she sees his upper body moving in small circles with each note. The hollow, breathy sounds are steady like a ticking clock, and they sound somewhat familiar.

Suddenly the melody stops. An uneasy silence follows, and the man lowers the flute.

Though his eyes are still hidden under the rim of the hat, Allison can tell that he is watching her, close. He places the flute on the hood, stands up, and slips his hands into his coat pockets.

"Hello?" Allison asks, and she is surprised by the thin, fragile sound of her voice.

The man doesn't say anything or move an inch. She is about to speak again—this time with her What's-your-problem? voice—when he starts toward her with slow, deliberate steps.

There is something ominous about his body now. He moves as if he knows he can catch her no matter what. The courage drains right out of her, and Allison realizes that this isn't a game.

Maybe he had something to do with Harold and now he's after her, too, she thinks in a panic.

Crunch, crunch, crunch . . .

Her heart is racing now. She tries to move her legs but can't at first. It's as if the gravel has become quicksand. She can feel the sweat on the backs of her legs, and her breathing gets short and hard. The scarf seems to tighten around her neck. The man is only a few feet away now, getting closer with each step.

31

Crunch, crunch, crunch . . .

An image of the man who killed her sister—still standing over her lifeless body—breaks Allison from the trance. She gets to the door and yanks it open.

"What the hell," she mutters, keeping her eye on the door as she steps backward into the chapel.

She expects the man to burst through at any second, to grab her, to squeeze the air from her with his knotted hands. Her body tenses. She can feel her throat tighten and her heart crash like thunder. She stops moving, waiting and looking around at the people sitting quietly inside. They don't seem to notice her.

Ten seconds pass. . . .

Twenty . . . forty-five . . .

Sixty . . .

Nothing. The door doesn't rattle or shake or swing open. The man doesn't appear. Everything is quiet.

Allison exhales for the first time in what feels like forever, and once again she looks around Cicely's Funeral Home.

The cool darkness feels safe somehow. *Safer.* It has been a long time since she has been here. At best, the place makes a halfhearted attempt at being a chapel—the two stained-glass windows at the front don't let in much light on cloudy days, and the white benches remind her more of cheap lawn furniture than of church pews. It is quiet except for her thudding heart, and the whole place smells of old things, mothballs, and layers of dust.

The chapel is mostly empty. An older woman sits near the front. Her shoulders are straight and hard, not curled forward in grief, and Allison wonders if that is Harold's foster mother, Ms. Wilton. Three other people are in the front row, two dark-haired girls and a tall boy with narrow shoulders. Allison immediately thinks of Jade, Emma, and David. *They've come back too,* she tells herself, but she isn't sure. She hasn't seen them in so long that she's afraid to go up there. Sheriff Cooper stands at the back. He hasn't changed one bit since her days in Meridian. He's almost as round as he is tall, and his stomach still pushes out against his brown uniform as if it's ready to make a break for it. Sheriff Cooper nods to Allison, and she smiles back—not as a greeting or because she's happy to see him. She's definitely *not* happy to see the man who shoved her and her friends into police cars five years ago and shipped them to different parts of the country. No, her feelings about Sheriff Cooper fall somewhere between hating his guts and hating his guts, but she smiles out of relief—relief, perhaps for the first time in her life, that a cop is nearby.

Allison doesn't have any more time to wonder about the people in the front row before the side door swings open with a swoosh. There is a flash of white light. Allison squints, and her stomach seems to drop to her knees.

It takes a few seconds to realize who's there. It's not the man from outside, the man who moves like a hunter of people. It's Ike Dempsey, breezing toward her with a swagger. His bright orange hair sticks up like he just rolled out of bed, and his blue eyes remind her of the Carolina skies in springtime. Ike's face is still narrow and kind and sprinkled with freckles, and he walks right up to her as if no time has passed since they last saw each other.

"You just gonna stand around all day or what?" he asks with a smirk before plopping into the nearest bench.

Allison sits next to him, still a bit shaky and dazed from the scare. She also can't believe her eyes. Ike Dempsey. After all the time she spent trying to forget, she started wondering if her old life didn't exist at all, and now it's only six inches away. She wants to poke him in the shoulder—just to be sure he's really real—but instead she blurts out, "Did you see that guy outside?"

"What guy?"

"In the parking lot . . . by the crappy car? I saw him after I pulled in."

Ike shakes his head, and Allison can tell from the look on his face that he thinks she's one step away from the loony bin. But instead of asking her what kind of medication she's on, he whispers, "This totally sucks."

"What?"

"Having practically no one show up," he says, looking around the room and fidgeting in his seat. "How do you think Tom Sawyer would've felt if only seven people showed up to his funeral?"

Allison can tell that Ike is just talking foolish to hide his nerves, but she understands. She hasn't felt right ever since being back in Meridian—the town circle, the cemetery, the man in the parking lot, and even this cheap funeral parlor. It all feels a bit unreal.

And dangerous.

"At least we're here," she offers, but Ike only shrugs.

Allison glances around the chapel and realizes that he's right. More people should be here—crying or blowing their noses or falling over with grief. Sad music should be playing in the background. Instead the building is quiet as a library.

Allison wonders about her own funeral. With Mel and Daddy and Ma gone, who would show up? Heather would find a way to get there. Allison spends most of her meaningful time with Heather—after school at the mall or just hanging around Insomnia, the wannabe Starbucks on Kingston Street. Bo works there. He may not be the sharpest knife in the drawer, but he can kiss in a way that warms your whole body. During breaks they hang out in the back, kiss, share cigarettes, and sip from their free café mochas.

Yeah, Bo would probably make it to her funeral, but

Allison doesn't think he'd miss her for long. Sure, his touch makes her happy, and she likes the way he kisses deep, because you have to be completely in the moment for that kind of kissing. But Bo isn't her forever someone. From their very first kiss she has known something is missing. Some feeling that should be there.

Maybe Sheriff Cooper would show up to her funeral, she considers next, but no one else from Meridian, that's for sure. She can picture Mr. and Mrs. Packer wearing black and sitting by her coffin, but she can't imagine them crying. Not that they wouldn't be sad. Allison is pretty sure that Mrs. Packer and Brutus Packer Jr. would miss her. But being sad and weeping from real pain are different things.

No, Allison can't think of one person who would cry hard, painful tears for her like she has for Mel, and that makes her realize something: She's no Tom Sawyer. She would never risk going to her own funeral.

It'd be way too depressing.

A tall man in a flowing black gown appears from a small door at the front of the chapel and approaches the podium. The yellowish wood of the coffin seems cheap and flimsy to Allison. Next to it, on a small table, there is a black-and-white photograph of Harold.

She recognizes the smile on Harold's face. He would get that expression after scurrying up trees faster than anyone else. That's when he was happiest. Away from Jacob and his words . . .

"The outside world knows only corruption and intolerance, violence and hatred," he preached. "We have chosen a different path. A divine path. Most other folks don't understand, as we do, that the time is near, that every hour, every minute, every second, it gets closer. And we need to prepare. We need to distinguish ourselves from the lot, to show our readiness to be leaders in the next life."

Allison tries to push Jacob's voice out of her head. The rise and fall of it, the changing rhythms . . . it has a way of sticking with you. Sometimes she hears him in her dreams, as if he's lying right next to her, whispering.

"We are gathered here today to mourn the loss of Harold Crawley," the preacher begins flatly, as if he's reading from note cards for the first time. "It always seems particularly sad when a young person dies. But . . ." The preacher pauses to look out at the group.

"But let's face it," Ike whispers, mimicking the preacher and leaning close to Allison. "You're all going soon. So get used to it."

Ike laughs nervously, but Allison can't bring herself to join in. Some things cut too close to the bone for laughing. She looks at the preacher again, pretending to listen, but instead of his voice she only hears Jacob's final promise:

"In five years' time, your greatest fear will consume you. It will rob you of your last breath."

For the first time all day Allison remembers her vision of Harold in black green waters. Screaming where no one could hear. Drowning.

What if Jacob is responsible somehow?

No, Allison tells herself. It's not possible. Jacob's dead. Someone else drowned Harold and dragged him into the tobacco field. Someone brought him to Meridian so that Allison and the other survivors would come back. That must be it.

But why?

The service ends as quickly as it began. The preacher makes the sign of the cross to no one in particular and retreats to the door at the front of the chapel. Everything gets quiet, until one of the girls in the front row steps into the aisle. It's Jade Rowan. Her raven hair has streaks of blue, matching her eyeliner and nail polish, and the silver rings on her hands make them look thick. Her black skirt stops several inches above her knees, and she wears high black leather boots. She walks right up to Allison and Ike.

"Hey." Her voice is softer than her look, and this reminds Allison of the Jade she knew from five years ago. Quiet, scary smart, and never far from a piano. She liked Beethoven and Liszt the best. Big pieces with big sounds. Even back then Allison could tell that Jade enjoyed shocking folks. No one could believe such a tiny body could make so much sound, and almost every jaw in Jacob's congregation dropped clear to the floor the first time she played.

Allison doesn't know what to say, so she gives Jade a hug. Wrong move. She can feel Jade's body get stiff, and Allison lets go. She's not sorry, though. It feels more right than talking.

David Holloway and Emma Caulder are right behind Jade. Emma stands back from the rest of them. Her thick glasses seem too wide for her face, and she mostly stares at the floor. Her bangs cover her forehead like one of those soapy curtains at a car wash, and her baggy black sweater gives her body a shapeless quality. Under it she wears a loose black dress that hangs to the floor.

"Hi," David says hoarsely, and his voice sends a chill down Allison's back.

David is taller than the rest of them by at least six inches, and Allison has to tilt her head to see his hazel eyes with golden flecks. He has wavy brown hair and a narrow nose that makes his face look serious but not too serious. He loosens his tie and then lets his long arms fall to his sides. He's uncomfortable, not just because no one knows what to say to one another, but because his suit is way too small. The jacket sleeves stop a couple inches above his wrists, and the collar of his shirt appears to be strangling him. But this only makes him more cute, Allison thinks. More handsome.

"I gotta get out of this damn thing," David says to everyone. "I haven't worn it in two years."

"Let's go. I have some booze back at the hotel," Jade pipes up. "I say we drink."

"Hell yes," Ike chimes in, and Allison can feel him standing close to her, his body almost touching hers.

"Dave and I will lead the way," Jade continues. "We're staying at the Winds. Room twelve."

Together? Allison practically blurts out, but she manages to keep her mouth shut. Thankfully. Allison didn't think much about where she'd stay once she got to Meridian. She didn't know what to expect—if anyone else would show up to the service or if she could find out more about Harold's death here. She dreaded the idea of coming back and didn't want to think about staying. That changed once she saw David—though she sure doesn't like the sound of Jade's "Dave and I," as if they've been planning a vacation to the Bahamas.

Before anyone else can speak, Sheriff Cooper's big belly pushes its way into their circle.

"It was nice of y'all to come," he says in a strained whisper, as if to remind them that they're in a chapel. "I'm sure Harold would've been very appreciative." Sheriff Cooper squints with each word, and Allison wonders if he needs glasses. He hesitates before adding, "Are y'all planning to stay around long?"

"Why the hell would we do that?" Jade snaps before turning to David. "Let's go."

Jade doesn't wait for a response before storming toward the side door. She slaps it open with both hands and disappears into the parking lot. The sheriff's face gets slightly red, but whether it's from embarrassment or just being plain annoyed, Allison can't tell.

"Well . . . ," he begins again, "I've gotta tend to Ms. Wilton."

With that, Sheriff Cooper steps over to Harold's foster mother. She hasn't moved since Allison's arrival, but when he puts his hand on her shoulder, she bows her head and starts to weep quietly.

"Do you guys need a ride? We all came from the hotel together," David says to Allison and Ike, but she wonders if he's really just asking her. He still has that sweetness that made her want to kiss him a long time ago—one summer afternoon in the old tree house.

But before she can respond, Ike says, "No, that's cool. I'll go with Allison. And Emma, you can come back with us if you want."

"Didn't you drive here yourself?" Allison snaps.

"No," Ike replies, unfazed. "I took a cab from the train station. Besides, I think it's better to travel in packs."

Outside the mist has gotten thicker and colder. Allison looks around for the man with the flute but doesn't see him or the rust-colored car anywhere. This doesn't make her feel any better, though.

She has never been comfortable with disappearing acts.

Jade's red Jeep is idling by the exit, and she honks twice, leaning partway out of the window. David turns to Allison one more time.

"See you there, right?" he asks.

"Yeah, do you want my cell—"

"There's no reception."

"What?" Ike blurts out, taking the phone from his back pocket and checking for himself.

"Jade and I haven't been able to get a signal anywhere in town," David adds.

Allison glances at her own cell phone. Nothing.

"This totally sucks," Ike says. He steps away from them,

holding up his phone, still looking for reception.

Jade honks again.

"I better go. See you there," David says to Allison before jogging to the passenger side of the Jeep, pulling himself inside, and speeding away in a cloud of gray dust.

The sound of the Jeep fades away almost as quickly.

Ike snaps his phone closed and pauses.

"So . . . ," he says, looking at the Barracuda in the center of the lot. "That must be yours."

"Yep," Allison says absently. She isn't in the mood for old-car jokes right now, so she doesn't encourage him. Even though her head is spinning with thoughts of David and the strangeness of seeing all her old friends, there is something she has to do first. Something that can't wait.

Allison walks past her car toward the cemetery. The sign at the entrance reads: REMEMBER. But she doesn't think that needs much reminding, though. It's forgetting that's the hard part.

"Where are you going?" Ike calls out.

Allison turns partway around and sees him standing there with his palms up, as if he's about to catch something. Emma waits behind him, looking at her feet.

"To see my sister," Allison says.

4

BLOOD ATONEMENT

Mel's grave is just like Allison remembers it. She was worried that it might be overgrown with weeds or wildflowers, but the gardeners here keep the grounds up nice. They're a lot cleaner than Allison's room at the Packers' house, that's for sure. Mel's name, etched in white against the black stone, is clear as crystal, not scratched up or faded like on some of the older graves, and there are even a few fresh flowers by the headstone.

It doesn't feel right having Ike and Emma standing behind her. Ike fidgets like he has to pee, so Allison cuts the visit short. *I'll come back,* she says to herself and to Mel. *I promise.*

With that, she leaves the cemetery.

Allison is still annoyed with Ike. He's acting like there's something between them, like he did when he gave her that dreamcatcher years ago. He's acting like a boy with a crush.

Maybe I'm no better, Allison admits to herself. It took her less than one tenth of a second to get a butterfly stomach in front of David and to think about the day that they almost kissed. Allison isn't sure if those feelings and daydreams are love. Maybe loving someone is natural as the way a person laughs. It comes from somewhere inside, and you just can't change it.

Allison unlocks the car. Emma climbs into the passenger seat, and Ike slides into the back. In the rearview mirror Allison can see him fidgeting again—his head nodding as if music were pumping through the speakers. Allison wonders if he is ever still, but from the looks of it, she doesn't think so.

They all stay quiet as Allison starts up the car. Gravel grinds beneath the tires as they pull away from Cicely's Funeral Home and start down the rough, uneven path toward the highway. Emma folds her pale hands in her lap. Her shoulders curl slightly forward, and she seems to be studying something on the floor.

"So, Emma . . . ," Allison begins after a few minutes, though she still isn't sure what to say. "How are things going?"

Ike laughs, and pretty soon Allison and Emma join in. Maybe it's the ridiculous question or the weirdness of being back in Meridian or not knowing whether to be sad or scared because of Harold's death. Allison isn't sure, but it doesn't matter. The laughter feels good.

It *sounds* good too.

"Things are fine," Ike says through a cough. "I've spent five years in Cults Anonymous and haven't missed a meeting. Of course, my sponsor tells me that I get a little negative when I talk about the end of the world. But other than that, I'm fine. . . . How are you?"

Emma covers the smile on her face with both hands, and she leans back in the seat. Tears gather in Allison's eyes, and she can't remember the last time she cried from something other than sadness.

The laughter fades in a few moments, and though they're silent again for a while, it isn't awkward like before.

"Seriously," Allison tries again, her voice still light from laughing. "What are you up to now?"

Emma begins tentatively, like a turtle poking its head out of a shell. She goes to Immaculate Conception High School and spends the rest of her time volunteering for a local library. School is boring. But school and learning are different things, and most of her classes aren't hard at all.

"I mean, we were doing tougher math problems and studying more history and stuff with Jacob than most seniors do at my high school," Emma says with a touch of pride.

Allison remembers all the hours of schooling at the compound. They worked from eight thirty in the morning to three in the afternoon, just like normal school, except with breaks for lunchtime prayers and afternoon meditation. Since there were only six kids, you had to carry your own weight in every class and with every assignment. The Doctor handled all the science and math classes. He was patient and soft voiced and a lot nicer than Jacob when you slacked off. Jacob taught everything else—religion and English and history and philosophy. They read Socrates and Sartre, Dickens and Shakespeare. Basically, they read until their brains hurt, like when you eat ice cream too fast and the chill goes to your head.

Emma's sure right about one thing, Allison thinks. *All that work has made high school a breeze.*

"Of course, my foster parents think something's up because I spend so much time away from home," Emma continues. "They figure I'm one step away from being a drug dealer or a prostitute or even a Catholic. I don't know . . . maybe it'd be easier for them if I started dealing drugs. Proof positive that I'm the screwup they always thought I'd turn out to be. Instead, they go to church three times a week to pray for me, and Mrs. Weaver, my foster mom, gets so upset about all the books in my room that she calls them 'the devil's dictation.'"

"The devil's dictation?" Allison echoes incredulously, about ready to burst out laughing again.

"Yeah, it's hard to believe how stupid stupidity really is," Emma says flatly, without a hint of humor. "Basically, she's never read a book in her life, so she figures that anything in them has to be bad."

Emma's world couldn't be more different from Allison's.

Classes and libraries are the last things Allison would talk about. Not that she doesn't do well in school. She got an A on Mr. Bernstein's chemistry midterm, and she hardly gets any red marks on her English papers. But school isn't where her heart is.

It's clear that Emma's big love affair is with the Lynchburg Public Library. Checking out books. Working in the stacks. Ordering from the catalog. Helping the patrons find what they're looking for even when they don't have the first clue. And when it comes to libraries, Emma isn't shy about talking at all.

"'Do you have something on the solar system?' It always starts that way," Emma says eagerly, "but you gotta ask the right questions to find the right books. That's what I do. I help people ask the right questions, instead of telling them what to do."

"You must really like to read," Ike says, and Allison can hear the utter boredom in his voice, as if he'd rather be sentenced to life in prison than spend one hour in a library, let alone work in one.

"I love books," Emma says, then pauses to think. "They're just what they seem to be."

Emma gets quiet, and for the first time Allison understands. Books do have a certain honesty to them. What you see is what you get. And in that way they're everything that Jacob wasn't. . . .

When Jacob caught Allison trying to take the golden box from his room, she expected to go to the Confessional. She had broken one of the rules—well, several rules, actually. She'd lied, pretending to be sick so she could leave evening prayer service early and sneak into Jacob's room. Then she got caught stealing the box where Jacob kept things from each child's past. For Allison, it was her epilepsy medication and a silver locket with Mel's picture inside. She used to wear it around her neck.

So Allison had committed a double whammy of sin in less than five minutes. She knew she'd have to pay a price, but when she was thrown into the pit, she didn't expect to see the end of the world that day.

Allison hit the dirt floor of the pit. Hard. Suddenly her body burned all over. Hot coals were biting into the palms of her hands, her breasts, her stomach, her knees. Everywhere.

She tried to scramble away from the glowing cinders, half crawling and half rolling until she hit something. A wall. She got to her feet fast. Clouds of hot, strangling smoke were everywhere. She covered her mouth with one hand, but she had already swallowed mouthfuls. She could feel it.

Allison moved along the uneven stone wall, guiding herself with one hand. The pit was getting warmer, and her head started to spin. She stumbled from the dizziness and confusion. Tears streamed down her cheeks.

Then she fell again—this time through an opening in the wall. The air felt cooler here, as if she had fallen into a room or passageway of some kind. She stayed on her knees for a moment, trying to breathe through the smoke and her own coughing.

That's when she heard the growling. It seemed to be all around her—hungry and fierce.

She struggled to see through the grayness, but shadows moved everywhere in the smoke. She had to get away, to run . . . even if it was right into the mouth of a lion.

The growling surged. Allison got to her feet, wobbling unsteadily. But before she could take her first step, something grabbed her hair and pulled. Her head tilted back with a sudden jerk, and an icy coolness slid across her neck, quick and even.

Whatever had grabbed her disappeared in a flash. She fell

to the ground, her body folding in on itself like a discarded puppet. Her heart was sputtering. A palpable fear pulsed through her.

She was okay, though. She could make it out of there, she told herself. She was sure of it.

But something *was* wrong. Allison couldn't get up. She touched her throat where the cold had been and felt a thick warmness spilling down the front of her body. It covered her hands and dripped onto her wrists and forearms.

Blood. Everywhere.

Her throat had been cut, and she was bleeding bad. It was pouring out of her. The room was getting darker, and then she realized something. . . .

She was going to die.

That's the last thing she remembers thinking before passing out. . . .

She woke up in the infirmary, a small room with only two beds and a narrow window that looked out onto the compost heap. It smelled rotten and dirty all the time. Thick bandages were wrapped around Allison's neck, tight enough to make it hard to move, and her throat felt desert dry.

The Doctor was the only one allowed to visit her. He brought glasses of water with colorful straws and books that were more fun than what they read for Jacob—Agatha Christie mysteries and *Dr. Jekyll and Mr. Hyde*.

"Jacob said that you were running away from your penance, that you fell into the ravine," the Doctor said one day, after she had been in the infirmary for more than a week. "Jacob had to climb down there to get you, to carry you back. You hurt yourself pretty bad."

The Doctor cut one side of her bandages with a pair of long, shiny scissors and lifted the bandages off in long strands.

Each one was stained brown and yellow and red. "You shouldn't have done that, Al."

Allison was shocked. *How can someone be so kind and so stupid at the same time?* she thought angrily. The Doctor had taken her to the Confessional in the first place. He knew what had happened. This was his fault too.

The Doctor unwound a new strand of gauze, but before he put it on her neck, Allison pointed to the wound.

"You think I got this from falling?" she said hoarsely, but the Doctor didn't look. He just closed his black eyes for a moment and exhaled.

"Sometimes we have to atone for our sins with blood," he said as he laid the clean dressing on her neck. It felt cool and soft against her skin.

Allison had heard all of this before from Jacob. "Blood atonement," Jacob called it. But the Doctor didn't have Jacob's sinister poetry in his voice. He just sounded a bit sad and lost. Still, Allison couldn't figure out why Jacob had let her live, why he had come so close to killing her, then stopped.

"You're going to be just fine," the Doctor said all of a sudden, but Allison wondered if he was trying to convince her or himself. "Jacob forgives you."

The Doctor finished dressing the wound and left the infirmary without another word. Allison had another twelve days to think about what had happened to her and what the Doctor had said. About what truth she discovered that day.

Before it was all over, Jacob would terrorize all of them. They would all be made to atone with blood and fire. And even though Allison didn't realize it then, she had seen a glimpse of the end of the world that day. The end of the Divine Path. The end that Jacob had been planning for them all along.

5

THE WAKE OF
HAROLD CRAWLEY

Along Route 54 the sign for the Whispering Winds Hotel can be seen for almost a mile in either direction. It peers above the line of trees like someone looking for a seat in a crowded movie theater. In fact, the sign is the highest point in Meridian, and it is made higher by the fact that the hotel is perched on the town's only hill. *"Hill" might not be the right word*, Allison thinks as she drives up the gentle slope. *"Hotel" might not be the right word either.* Fifteen rooms, no continental breakfast, and no HBO. That doesn't sound like much of a hotel to her, but it's the only place to stay for miles.

The Whispering Winds got its name from the high-pitched whistling sounds that whip through the doors and poorly insulated windows late at night. It doesn't take more than a breeze to get the whole place singing, and the folks in Meridian used to joke that it was near impossible to sleep through the night there.

"It's the perfect place to send your in-laws," Sutter Jones would tell his customers at the pharmacy, and the grown-ups always laughed at that, no matter how many times they'd heard it.

Allison pulls into the parking lot, and even in the twilight the Whispering Winds looks like a dump—cracked, faded paint and a paper-thin rooftop. She wouldn't be surprised if the whole place just fell over one day—exhausted from so many years of neglect.

"Camelot," Ike mutters as they get out of the car. He

stands with his hands on his hips, looking at the flickering neon sign overhead.

They start looking for room 12, but the numbers don't follow any logical order—7, 3, 9, 6. . . . Allison wonders if it is some kind of prank, if some guest—angry and sleepless from the whistling winds—decided to rearrange them one night.

"I thought I sucked at math," Ike mutters without slowing his pace, and Emma falls in step behind him, close enough to be his shadow.

Allison wonders if Ike gives her the butterfly stomach.

Probably.

As they turn the corner, Allison sees the rust-colored car from the funeral, and it stops her cold. That man again. There are no other cars in the lot. Just *his*, parked near a pile of cardboard boxes and a Dumpster. She looks for the man, her heart racing once again.

Nothing.

A light breeze pushes through the trees, and for a second Allison thinks she hears a faint melody. Her throat starts to tighten. Ike and Emma are several doors ahead of her now, and Allison considers yelling out to them. But to say what, exactly?

"Watch out for freelance flute players?"

"Speed kills?"

No, there's nothing to say because there's nothing here, she admits. No melody lingers in the wind. No one leans against the hood. There is only an empty car and some trash.

Ike reaches the other end of the lot and calls out to Allison, "What's up?"

She shakes her head and then hurries past several rooms to catch up: 1, 5, 15, 4. . . .

At the back of the hotel Jade's red Jeep is parked in front of room 12. Like every other side of the building, the room faces out onto miles of dense trees, and Allison wonders how anyone decided to build something here. So isolated. So closed off from the rest of the world.

Ike knocks on the door twice.

"Enter," Jade says, swinging open the door, and she hands him a beer.

The room is one bad motel cliché after another—a cheap particleboard desk with a matching dresser, gray carpets, floral wallpaper, and a lumpy bed with a multicolored comforter that, as far as Allison can figure, is trying to achieve a whole new level of ugliness. David sits by the nightstand, searching for a radio station on the alarm clock there. The sight of him on the bed bothers Allison. She wonders if maybe he is staying with Jade after all, if they hooked up as soon as they found their way back to Meridian. Or worse—if they reconnected long before now and are together.

Seriously together.

Jade plops down on the bed next to David, leaning against the wooden headboard and stretching her legs out in front of her. She picks up the open beer on the nightstand and takes a long gulp.

As soon as she comes up for air, she says, "There's more in the fridge."

Ike takes a seat in the chair by the desk, and Allison can tell that he's staring at Jade's legs. Emma slinks past them, but instead of getting a drink, she drops into the puffy chair on the other side of the room.

The hissing from the clock radio stops, and a faint song without words crackles through the speaker. It sounds like the jazz that Daddy used to listen to after supper. Every night he'd tune the stereo to the same jazz station, pick up a newspaper, and sit in his favorite chair. Its worn leather was the softest thing Allison had ever touched, even softer than Ma's hair after it was clean and she'd brushed it straight. Sometimes Allison would sit in his lap, and he'd read something to her before bedtime. But that was before they gave up the house and everything in it to become followers of Jacob.

"This is the only station I can find," David complains softly, and he turns to everyone with an apologetic smile, as if he's to blame for the bad reception. He has changed into a pair of jeans and a black T-shirt that hugs his chest. Allison can see that he's more muscular than she first thought, more muscular than Bo.

"No thanks on the elevator music," Jade says, and Ike laughs in that polite way boys laugh when they're hot for you.

"It's not elevator music. It's Miles Davis," Emma corrects. Her eyes flutter at Ike, but he doesn't notice.

"Who?" Jade asks after another sip.

"Never mind," Emma replies, downcast. With Ike staring at Jade's legs, and the rest of them not having the first clue about Miles Davis, Emma slumps farther into her chair in defeat.

David turns off the radio and stays seated on the bed, close to Allison and Emma. The squareness of his face reminds Allison of those marble statues in museums. Heroes and gods and warriors carved in stone. Handsome. Strong.

"Do you think . . ." Allison's voice cracks, and she begins again. "Do you think it's safe here?"

"In the hotel?" Ike asks sarcastically, his eyes still on Jade.

"No, in Meridian."

"It's safe enough," Jade says sharply.

"How do you know?" Allison asks.

"Look," Jade begins, leaning her head back and glancing at the stained ceiling, "what happened to Harold sucks. But that doesn't mean we have to relive everything. What's done is done."

Allison hesitates. "But what if it's not done?"

Jade shakes her head, then takes a long sip of beer.

Allison looks around the room, but everyone seems far away now. Eyes lowered. Fingers peeling the paper labels off beer bottles. Bodies shifting uncomfortably. No one speaks. Until seeing all of them together again, Allison didn't realize how dangerous coming back to the funeral might be. Maybe she came back to Meridian to convince herself that that danger was just in her head, that everything would be okay and that Harold's death was a strange accident, not a portent. Maybe that's why they all came back. To lie to themselves a little longer. But now she is convinced that something is wrong.

"So . . . ," Jade says, turning her attention to Ike. Her forced, bright tone announces the change of subject. "What's your story?"

"My story?" Ike echoes, as if he'd rather not be distracted from looking up her skirt.

"Yeah, your story," she continues with a smirk, watching him watch her and basking in it. "What you've been up to for, I don't know, the last *five* years? And don't give us some one-minute, G-rated version. We want the real deal."

Ike mutters through some general things at first—about recently dropping out of high school and not getting along with his foster parents. But once Jade rolls her eyes, he shifts gears and starts talking about airplanes.

"I know lots of people who are afraid of flying—afraid because they can't think about anything other than the fall. But all sorts of things can happen at thirty thousand feet," he explains. "Turbulence. Electrical storms. Air pockets. Crying babies. That's the whole point. Flying is about taking chances. It's about letting your feet off the ground."

Ike leans forward in his chair, closer to Jade. "To see people and cars from the tops of buildings is one thing.

But to be so far up that you can look down on clouds— *clouds*—now, that's just badass."

Almost every part of Ike's life seems to involve defying gravity. He tells them that he just started working on the tallest buildings and handling the toughest inclines for Mountain High Cleaners. That he never loses his footing on a slick surface. Not even close. He practically started the company, anyway. Well, his buddy Jake came up with the money and manages the business side of things. But it was Ike's idea to specialize in office buildings and skyscrapers.

Technically, Ike doesn't turn eighteen for another few months, but Jake fudged the books so he could get started early. They first met on the rock-climbing wall at Arnold's Gym, so Jake knows that Ike can handle standing on a wooden plank forty stories above the asphalt. That Ike can keep his balance when the winds start whipping at his body. No problem.

He pauses to sip his beer. "The bottom line is—I love every minute of it."

This should come as no surprise, though, Allison thinks. After all, his full name—Icarus—is all about flying.

She has never forgotten the story of his parents. He told it many times when they all lived at the compound. The Dempseys were traveling in Greece when they first found out the news: Elena, his mom-to-be, was pregnant. They had been trying to have a baby for a long time, so this was good news. His parents were so excited that they wanted to name their son something important, something special. But they couldn't make up their minds until the day he was born.

Only when his dad was holding him for the first time, looking down at that bright orange hair and aerodynamic body (his father was an engineer before they started living with the Divine Path), did he name his son: Icarus. The nurses looked at him funny, but as he told Ike much later,

"It was just the first word that popped out of my mouth."

So that's how Ike was named after some guy in Greek mythology who liked to fly. Apparently, Icarus flew so high that he almost touched the sun—before the wax on his wings melted and he fell into the sea and drowned.

Allison doesn't like flying herself. She'll do it, but she'd rather be behind the wheel of a car, where you can change course with just a turn and where the tires never leave the ground. Driving is all about taking control—leaving when you want, going where you want, and stopping when you want along the way.

Right now Allison wants David. To talk. She wants to ask him about *his* life and all the missing time between them. But not here, not in front of everyone else. She tries to imagine what his voice sounds like up close in the dark—when you're talking to someone in sweet whispers and you can smell the mix of soap and sweat on his body. The good kind of sweat.

She also wants to know where he's sleeping tonight.

But before Allison has a chance to ask David anything, Jade decides to talk about her busy social calendar—though Allison can't remember anyone asking.

"My boyfriend back in the city doesn't like heights. He's kind of a wuss that way. But Silo isn't much better. . . ."

By "the city," Jade means Washington, D.C. By "boyfriend," Jade means one of three guys who seem entirely interchangeable in that department—Gene (a high school senior whose biggest claim to fame is a television commercial he did for Tide detergent at the age of seven), Silo (a violinist who played a concert with Jade last year and sneezed during the finale), and Danny (who lives in "the city" and supports himself by working as a supermarket cashier).

Jade doesn't talk much about school or her family up in Washington. She doesn't mention best friends, favorite movies, or annoying foster brothers. From the sound of it, you'd think she does only one thing—juggle guys. And as Allison watches how the names of Jade's boyfriends deflate Ike like needles in a balloon, she can tell that Jade has a serious talent for juggling.

Ike slumps back in his chair and grabs another beer. He takes longer swigs now as he listens to stories about Danny's narcolepsy and the time Gene got caught smoking a joint during lunch break at their high school. Allison listens too, but all she hears is a girl who knows how to perform—hiding behind funny stories and a tough attitude, talking without really saying anything.

Allison wonders if guys, like Ike, find her mysteriousness as sexy as her clothes. But Allison would rather get a glimpse of the real Jade. She has had enough of fast-talkers to last a lifetime.

"Yeah," Jade continues, "Gene doesn't seem to be able to do *anything* without some pot. Being mellow is, like, his whole thing—"

"Do you love any of them?" Emma blurts out, and everyone turns to her, surprised.

The words don't sound mean, but they stop Jade in her tracks. There is something about the sincerity of Emma's voice that sucks the air out of the room. She could have asked if Jade was just having sex with them, if it was nothing more than hormones and feeling good. Anyone could understand that. And Jade would probably have answered in her cool, hip, self-assured way. No sweat. But Emma asked about Love with a capital *L*. She said "love" like someone who has read every fairy tale ever written and is waiting her turn for castles and princes and white horses.

"I . . ." Jade hesitates, and the performer in her falters.

Allison completely understands. Love, with or without a

capital *L*, isn't the stuff of casual conversation. One day you have it, and you're driving everybody else crazy from showing it off too much—like Heather did when she was all over her first boyfriend before he dumped her for some theater chick at school—the next day it's gone. Someone steals it or you lose it. That's something Allison has learned. You can lose love just as easily as car keys or a cell phone. Some boyfriends cheat. Some mothers run away. But getting back lost love . . . well, that'll probably break your heart, Allison thinks—whether it's in little bits over time or all at once.

Jade finishes the rest of her beer in one fast chug and slaps the empty bottle on the night table. Her blue fingernails shimmer in the light. "What the fuck, Emma? We're just hanging out."

With that, Jade springs off the bed and grabs another beer from the fridge. Everyone is silent, and this is the first time since getting to the hotel that Allison can hear the whistling winds. They don't sing at all, she realizes. They start as a faint howling through the door—long, sustained, unnerving—and they get louder and louder, until you think you can't stand hearing them anymore.

And then they stop. All of a sudden.

This time the quiet in the room is nothing more than a pause before the next howl gets going. A chill runs up and down Allison's arms.

"So much for sleeping tonight," Ike mutters, but he says the words while staring at Jade, and Allison doubts that he's thinking about the whistling winds at all.

"Maybe . . . ," David begins tentatively, and stops to clear his throat. "Maybe we should have a toast or something for Harold. I mean, that's why we're here."

He holds up his beer, and everyone else does the same; even Emma grabs one of the empty bottles next to her.

"To Harold," David says, his voice kind and sincere, and each of them echoes the same before drinking.

Allison wonders what Harold would have been like after all these years—probably as different and awkward as everyone else tonight. Trying to move on changes a person, and that's what they've been doing. They've been living new lives with new families and new friends. They've been trying to forget the Jacob part of their past, but here they are. In Meridian all over again. It's like stepping into a time machine that only takes you back to the worst moments in your life, Allison thinks.

"So, are you staying a little while?" Ike asks Jade with a slight smirk on his face. "I hear the Meridian Cult Museum is worth a visit."

Jade holds the beer bottle close to her lips and blows into the rim until it wheezes like a foghorn. "Hell no. I'm outta here first thing tomorrow."

"You're leaving?" Allison asks, surprised.

"Ye-ah." Jade drags out the word as if she just heard the stupidest question in the world.

"What about Harold?"

"What about him?"

"Don't you think . . ." Allison hesitates, screwing up the courage to ask the question on her mind. "Don't you think it's strange that he drowned? That he died this year—the year Jacob said he would?"

"Not again," Jade mutters.

"You don't think it's strange?"

"He couldn't swim," Jade snaps, before blowing into the bottle again, and Allison can't decide which is more annoying—her smart-ass comment or the foghorn.

"Yeah, but they found him in a tobacco field," Allison presses.

"Whatever."

"*Whatever?*"

Jade leans forward aggressively. "What are you planning to do—make a vacation out of it? Or do you just want to hang out long enough to hook up with Dave?"

Allison can feel her cheeks burn with embarrassment, but she's not going to take the bait, she tells herself. She knows girls like Jade, always trying to impress guys with a big attitude and a short skirt.

"I think we should ask around a bit," Allison says, looking at everyone but Jade. "Find out what Harold was doing back here. If anyone had seen him around—"

"What for?" Jade snaps.

"Well . . ." Allison hesitates. "To be sure that Harold's death was an accident."

"O-kaaaay," Jade says, glancing at Ike and David. "You do realize that this isn't an episode of *CSI*, right?"

Allison shoots her a hard look before tuning to Ike, who is still slumped in the rickety desk chair by the fridge. "How did you find out about Harold?"

"What?" Ike asks, shifting uncomfortably in his seat.

"How did you hear about his death?"

"Look, I still can't believe my cell phone doesn't work—"

"Ike!"

"I don't know," he says. "I got an e-mail. A newspaper article."

"Forwarded from a stranger, right?" Allison turns to Jade. "What about you?"

Jade doesn't answer, but David does. "That's how I heard."

"Ditto," Emma says.

Allison faces Jade. "Do you think that's just another coincidence?"

Jade shrugs, her confidence fading.

"Whoever sent them wanted us to come back—"

"Wait a minute," David interrupts, moving toward the edge of the bed, closer to Allison and the puffy green chair that seems to be swallowing Emma. "You think someone wanted us *here*?"

Allison nods, looking at David's eyes. She sees a tiredness there that makes her wonder if the same kind of guilt keeps him up at night too. The winds start howling again, louder than before, and the sound is almost piercing. Ike marches over to the door and slams on it with the palm of his hand.

"Shut up!" he yells, before turning around to face Allison. "So, what are you saying?"

"They're coming true, aren't they?" Emma blurts out, using the thick arms of the chair to pull herself forward. "All the things Jacob said. They're going to happen to us."

"Bullshit!" Jade snaps.

"Why is it bullshit?" Emma asks. "Because you'd rather drink?"

"Now, that is the first good idea you've had all night." Jade reaches for the drawer of the nightstand and pulls out a bottle of tequila.

"What are we going to do?" Emma asks, her voice tense and high.

Allison wants to say something to Emma, to everyone, but she doesn't know what. Sometimes there just aren't words for things.

"What are we going to do?" Jade echoes as she takes out several plastic cups from the same drawer. She then opens the bottle and starts pouring. Allison can smell the sourness of the tequila almost immediately. It reminds her of Mexican restaurants and greasy fried beans.

"I'll tell you what I'm going to do," Jade continues as she passes around the cups. Even Emma takes one. "First I'm going to get drunk. Then I'm going to get the hell out of here tomorrow. I've spent too much of my fucking life thinking about God and Jacob and the end of the world. Not anymore."

Jade holds up a cup and takes the shot fast. Ike follows. Allison looks at David for a moment, and his eyes narrow. Allison drinks. The tequila burns her throat, and she sticks out her tongue from the sourness.

"Ugh." Allison shudders.

"Damn, I forgot something," Jade says as she gets off the bed and steps over to her suitcase. "Gene got me all this stuff as a going-away present," she explains, taking out a bag with several limes and a saltshaker.

She smiles and starts pouring the second round.

Eventually Allison loses count of the shots and the hours. It's nice to be so close to old friends, she thinks. To listen to everyone laughing and telling stories. To be surrounded by the people who understand what it was like with Jacob, who live with the memories of what happened. Even Emma is drinking—reluctant at first and then eager, like she's racing someone.

Soon the room gets dark. The low-watt lightbulbs seem to get weaker as the night goes on, and without wanting to, Allison can feel herself being pulled into sleep. The voices around her fade. . . .

She wakes up, startled. The light still glows, but no one is moving. Jade and Ike have passed out on the comforter of the bed. Their bodies face opposite directions, and Ike's hand touches her ankle. David is stretched out on the floor beside the bed. Allison slumps in the puffy chair. She glances around for Emma but doesn't see her. Everything gets dark again. . . .

Later the howling winds half wake her. They seem distant and close all at once. As she listens, they remind her of fire engines. The Packers live near a firehouse, and Allison has gotten used to the way sirens start far off and get louder before dropping away.

Soon the howl changes into a melody. A hollow, breathy tune.

Allison is almost certain that it's the sound of a flute. . . .

6

THE WATERLESS WELL

The horse looks as dusty as the road. Its rider slumps forward in the saddle, and the reins dangle loosely from her pale white hands. The gray sky overhead rumbles with storm clouds. It is a mean, hungry sound.

Then a flash. Fire from the sky, scorching the rider's face. Her skin burns red, and her eyes go coal black. She screams as her body falls hard to the ground. Smoke rises from the empty spaces where her eyes used to be.

She screams again, but the sound is swallowed by thunder.

There is no rain, just dryness and crying without tears. The ground shakes—

Allison wakes with a jolt. David is right in front of her, holding her hand. Stubble dots his chin and the sides of his face. Ike stands next to him, and his orange hair is even more disheveled than the day before. Jade hovers behind them, holding her forehead with one hand.

"Are you okay?" David asks. "You were shaking."

"I . . ." Allison tries to get up, but her head is still spinning from the seizure. She can taste blood in her mouth. "I'm fine. I just need my pills."

"Pills?" Jade's voice is as heavy as her eyelids.

"They're in my bag. In the car."

"I'll get them," David says, and he hurries out the door before she can say thanks.

Allison leans back in the puffy chair and closes her eyes to ease the dizziness. Her head throbs—some from the seizure, some from the tequila.

"I need an Advil," Jade mutters as she lumbers toward the bathroom. The faucet turns on with a snap, and Allison can picture her drinking from the spout.

"So . . . ," Ike mumbles, his voice hoarse and sleepy, "what happened?"

Allison opens her eyes and sees him sitting on the very edge of the bed, his feet tapping quietly against the floor and his fingers twitching.

"Sometimes I get the shakes when I dream. That's all."

"Like you used to for Jacob?"

Allison tilts her head back and exhales. "I guess. . . ."

All of the children met with Jacob in the early morning. He would come into the cabin and wake them with a start. Before sunrise. Before any of the adults were up.

"Rise," his voice boomed. "It's time to reveal what you've been seeing in your dreams. Every detail. Every image."

Then Jacob brought them to the waterless well—one at a time. The stone well had been there long before Jacob came to Meridian, but no one could get any water from it. Not a drop. It was just a dry hole in the middle of camp—a dry hole that made most folks thirsty. The way seeing something you don't have makes you want it even more.

"Close your eyes, Allison," Jacob began with a soft, sleepy voice. It was cold and damp in the early mornings, Allison remembers, but Jacob never seemed to notice. He was always warm enough for ten people. Sweating in his white linen suit as he spoke in front of the congregation. Turning red in the coolest weather. And fanning himself as he taught school. "I want to hear about your dreams."

Jacob asked Allison to talk more than anyone else, especially after her seizures. Her dreams were the most vivid then. Sounds and smells and faces. They were so real that sometimes Allison worried about getting lost in them forever. About never waking up.

That's why Jacob took away her medication. He wanted those dreams to continue. He was most interested when they were violent—filled with blood and fire, shadows and pain. Jacob's yellow eyes glistened when he heard these visions— that's what he usually called them, "visions." Every once in a while he'd touch her forearm or her knee. His hands clammy and moist with sweat. Allison wanted to pull away, but she was too afraid of what might happen.

"Praise be," he'd mutter before removing his hand and walking quickly to his cabin. "Praise be."

Even the memory of those words make Allison's chest feel tight.

The door of the room opens, and David rushes in with Allison's duffel bag. He wears the same jeans and black T-shirt from last night. His wavy hair is mussed in a way that makes her want to run her fingers through it. Just the sight of him makes her feel better. Calmer. Safer somehow.

"I brought the whole bag," he says, handing it to her.

Allison shuffles through it quickly, trying to hide most of what's inside. She doesn't want David to see her private things—underwear, bras, her retainer, which she is supposed to wear at night. *As if wearing braces for nineteen months wasn't bad enough,* she thinks. Allison finds the bottle of Tegretol at the bottom of the bag, takes it out, and cups it in her hand so no one can see the label.

"I should probably get something to eat," Allison says as she stands up slowly.

"Good. I'm fucking starved," Jade blurts out from the bathroom. "There has got to be a Denny's around here."

"Yeah, right," Ike says. "Or maybe a Hooters."

"Do they even serve breakfast?" David asks, playing along.

"Who cares?" Ike replies.

Allison turns to David. Her vision blurs somewhat, but at least she doesn't feel fall-over dizzy. "Where's Emma?"

"She went to her room last night—around two or so." David's body is so close that she could reach out and wrap her arms around him.

"She has her own room?"

"Yeah. So do I . . . I just didn't make it out of here last night."

Allison smiles. She is so relieved that David and Jade aren't together that she could do one of those dorky *Riverdance* numbers that Mrs. Packer likes to watch over and over again on DVD.

Suddenly the vision from this morning flashes before her. The pale woman on a horse. Her black hair falling to her shoulders. Eyes burning from a fire in the sky. That familiar face . . .

Allison shakes her head. "What room?"

"What?" David reaches out to touch her arm.

"What room is Emma in?" Allison's words are crisp, and David pulls back.

"Eleven, I think."

Allison can see the weirded-out expression on his face, but she doesn't have time to explain. She pushes past him and rushes out the door.

There are no whistling winds this morning, no winds at all. The sun is bright when it pushes through the scattered clouds, but it's not high enough to be warm yet. Allison hurries along the side of the building, unsteady and still somewhat off balance. She follows the random sequence of numbers—8, 10, 14, 2—until she finds 11.

She pounds on the door with one hand and uses the other

to lean against it for support. David and Ike rush up behind her.

"What are you doing?" David asks.

"I . . ." Allison thwacks the door again with her fist. "Emma's not answering."

"It's seven thirty," Ike mutters in a voice that sounds like he's rolling his eyes at the same time. "In the morning."

Allison turns to David. "We've gotta get in there."

"Okay . . . but—"

"Please," she says.

"I'll . . . I'll get the manager," David replies before jogging toward the front of the hotel.

Allison knocks on the door again. "Emma?"

Ike exhales audibly, as if he's too annoyed for words, and Allison turns.

"What?"

"Good question," Ike says impatiently. "What are you doing?"

"I'm worried about Emma—"

"Why?" Ike's steady, tired expression doesn't change.

"Why *what*?"

"Why are you worried about her? She probably passed out."

Allison leans back against Emma's door for balance. *Maybe Ike's right,* she thinks. Once Jade brought out the tequila last night, Emma started drinking with the rest of them. But not to fit in or to laugh louder or to make flirting with Ike easier. Allison could tell that Emma was drinking because of fear. Maybe they all were. Something about Jacob's prediction seemed to terrify Emma all over again—as if it was the first time she ever considered that it might come true, that she might be next.

"I . . . I saw her," Allison says. "In my dream."

"This morning?"

"Yeah. She was riding a horse and . . . lightning struck her."

"Lightning?"

Allison can hear the sarcasm creeping back into Ike's voice. She knocks on the door again. "It was Emma's face."

"I don't understand the big deal," Ike says.

"I saw Harold, too," Allison explains desperately. "Before I got the e-mail. I saw him drowning."

Allison's eyes sting with tears, and she turns away from Ike. She doesn't want dreams and seizures and the taste of blood in her mouth. She doesn't want her past to define her entire life—running away only to end up where she started. She has given enough to Jacob in blood and fear, that's for sure. She just needs Emma to be okay. She needs Jacob to be wrong about everything so she can go home.

Ike steps in close to her and tries the doorknob. The door opens slightly, but the chain stops it.

"Emma," Allison calls out, pressing her face close to the opening and trying to see inside.

"Move," Ike commands.

As Allison steps away, he throws his body, shoulder first, into the door. It swings open with a pop, and the broken chain falls heavily to the floor.

The early-morning sun lights only the entryway, leaving the rest of the room dark and shadowy. The curtains hang heavy and thick over the windows. The room smells of a smoldering campfire.

"Emma," Allison calls out as she steps inside.

It takes a few seconds before her eyes adjust and she can see Emma's body on top of the bed, white against the darkness. Emma wears only black panties and a matching bra. Her arms extend out from her sides, and her head is turned away from the door. Her long black hair hides most of her face.

Ike shouldn't see her like this, Allison thinks suddenly. He should wait outside. But before she can say anything, he snaps on the light. The weak bulb glows overhead, making everything a sickly yellow color.

"Emma?" Allison asks again, approaching the far side of the bed. "Are you all . . ."

Allison's words get lost in her sudden gasp for air. She can feel herself falling backward, knocking over the frail nightstand and the stack of books on top. She moves back against the wall, and something cracks loudly under her feet. She looks down: Emma's glasses. Ike is next to Allison now. He blinks repeatedly, and she can see the strength leaving his body.

Emma's face has deep, black caverns where her eyes should be. The skin around them is scorched black and red.

Allison's stomach turns as she realizes that the burning smell is from Emma's skin.

"Her eyes," Ike mutters. "They're gone."

7

STRANGERS

From the outside the Meridian Police Station doesn't look much like a police station. You'd walk right past it and never guess. The white pillars and big front porch remind most folks of the South you read about in history books. White masters in rocking chairs, drinking sweetened iced tea and fanning themselves. Slaves working in tobacco fields.

History always seems to be about two types of people, Allison thinks. Those who have power and those who don't.

Apparently the mayors of Meridian used to live in this house until 1981. In that year Kimball King, the mayor at the time, decided it was no longer appropriate for government officials to live in an old plantation house. So he gave it to the police and built a mansion with a swimming pool on the other side of town.

Allison wouldn't have known any of this if it weren't for the newspaper articles on the walls of the lobby, which is actually a den with a fireplace, cloth-covered chairs, and a not-so-comfortable couch. She is waiting for the sheriff to wrap things up with David and Ike and Jade. She wants to keep her mind busy, to stop herself from thinking about what she saw this morning.

Sheriff Cooper's questions weren't all that bad, Allison admits. He didn't act like those cops on television who lose their temper and throw someone against a wall. Sheriff Cooper never even raised his voice. He mostly asked the basics: "How was Emma acting at the party last night?" "Did she drink?" "What time did she leave y'all?" "What was she wearing?" "Was she upset about anything?"

But with each question Allison kept seeing Emma's unclothed body on the bed, eyes black and empty. Her body laid out like a crucifix.

Emma.

At the end of the interview he asked: "Is there anything else you can tell me about her?"

Allison hesitated. In truth, she couldn't think of a single thing. Not a phone number to call or the name of a best friend. Not a story about her new family or a cute guy at school. Nothing. After all these years Emma was just a stranger. They were all strangers to one another.

"She loved to read," Allison said at last. It was the best she could do.

He nodded. "Okay, then. Why don't you wait in the lobby and—"

"Sheriff?"

"Yes?"

"What happened?"

He stepped away from the table and opened the door for her. "We're trying to figure that out."

"Best guess," Allison pressed.

"Pardon?"

"Best guess about what happened?"

"I wish I knew." His voice was flat, almost sad, but his eyes narrowed as if making an accusation.

"You don't think I . . . that one of us—"

"You can wait in the lobby for your friends," he said.

The interview was over.

Friends?

Allison should have spit the word back at his pudgy face.

Sheriff Cooper had stolen her friends. He had cut them off from one another and sent them away, as if moving far distances could erase the past. Allison remembers crying herself to sleep for a long time after that. Sure, those tears came for lots of reasons—Daddy, Mel, Ma, and all the things that happened with Jacob. But losing her friends—her best friends—meant that she had no one left in the world.

She was totally alone.

Allison sits on the stiff couch in the lobby, her body still tired from the seizure and from being hungry. She feels a headache building.

"Hey," Ike says as he walks into the room. His voice has lost its breezy quality from yesterday.

"You okay?" Allison asks.

Ike shrugs as he plops onto the couch next to her. She can feel his leg shaking, but neither of them looks at each other. Allison figures it's better this way. It's not easy to look at someone when you're hurting. It makes it harder to hold back the tears somehow.

"Sheriff Cooper thinks one of us killed Emma," Allison says, and the gravity of this accusation hits her for the first time. She could go to jail. She could be sent away from everything she knows—again. No. She wraps her arms across her chest and squeezes tight, trying to stave off the panic.

Ike turns to her, his blue eyes shimmering and intense. "The windows were painted shut," he whispers. "They didn't open in Emma's room. I heard the manager telling the sheriff before we left."

"So?"

"So? The door was chained from the inside, and the windows didn't open. How could we have done it?" Ike's face reddens with frustration. He glances around the room before reaching into his pocket and pulling out a crumpled piece of paper. "I found this on the floor by her bed."

He hands the paper to Allison, and it feels moist and dirty from being in his pocket. She unfolds it carefully:

And now, behold, the hand of the Lord is
upon thee, and thou shalt be blind, not seeing
the sun for a season. And immediately there
fell on him a mist and a darkness; and he went
about seeking some to lead him by the hand.

Allison knows the story by heart. It was one of Jacob's favorites. Saul, a disbeliever, was traveling on the road to Damascus when God struck him with lightning and blinded him. Three days later his sight was restored, and he converted, changing his name to Paul.

Jacob saw himself as the bolt of light that lifted blindness from his followers. "We have all been blind to the truth at one time or another," he preached. "The truth is painful. It's not something all of us are ready to see. But there comes a day when we must take the road to Damascus.

"We must all be struck down to rise up again. . . ."

Ike sits forward now, watching Allison read. "Do you think it happened like that?"

"Like what?"

"With lightning. The way you saw it in your dream?"

"God doesn't leave notes," Allison mutters drily, trying to mimic Ike's sarcasm, but he doesn't seem to notice.

"Her books," Ike says softly, as if he's talking to himself. "I mean . . . that must be what she was most afraid of, right? Going blind." He pauses, and for the first time his body becomes still.

"I guess."

He doesn't speak.

"What is it?" Allison asks, uneasy about the faraway look in his eyes.

"Ever since this morning I've been thinking about Jacob's promise that we'd all die. Do you remember the day I went to the Confessional?"

For a long time Ike talked about it only in bits and pieces. Then one night he showed Allison the scars. She can still picture the shapes of the burn marks on his arms. They reminded her of constellations.

"Yeah." Allison's voice is soft. There are some things you can't forget.

No matter how hard you try.

Ike ran away from camp—but not for real, not for good. He just slipped out early one morning because he missed things. They all did. So Ike put on his jeans with the secret money pouch, which his mother had sewn there for summer camp years earlier, and he sneaked off to town for all of them. He was going to spend on them the only money he had kept hidden.

For Ike it was baseball cards and rock candy. Allison missed chocolate candy bars and root beer floats—but there was no way Ike could bring back a root beer float. Jade wanted some CDs, even though she had no way to play them. Piano music, mostly, and some Britney Spears. Emma asked for the newest Harry Potter book. And David . . . he didn't want anything. He didn't want Ike to get in trouble.

Jacob caught Ike on his way back from town, his mouth full of rock candy and a bag with goodies swinging from each arm.

Later that day Jacob would reveal that not all of them would be with him at the end. That the six children—all born in the same year—would die in the same year. That their deaths would signal God's plan for the end.

"On the day that the last of the six shall die, God will destroy the earth and all its wickedness with fire. He will begin again with a new garden and a new paradise. And the Chosen will be reborn as rulers and lawmakers.

"Praise be."

Still chewing candy, Ike stumbled back to camp, Jacob pulling him by the arm until they reached the Doctor's cabin.

"Take him to the Confessional for penance," Jacob ordered, before storming away with Ike's bags.

As always, the Doctor led Ike to the old shed, but this time he didn't speak. Not a word. The only sounds came from the woods and the dried leaves crunching under their feet.

At the Confessional the Doctor turned around and started back toward camp.

"Where are you going?" Ike called out, but the Doctor didn't answer. He just kept walking away.

Ike didn't know what to do, so he reached for the shed door to let himself in. That's when someone grabbed him from behind. A damp rag was pressed against his mouth.

Ike tried to pull it away, but the grip was heavy and solid like stone. A sweet smell filled Ike's nose. He kicked his legs and flung his arms about, trying to break free, but he couldn't breathe. His head started to spin. His arms dropped to his sides. Everything faded away. . . .

Ike woke up inside the smoky pit, cold and dizzy. His naked body strapped to a thick wooden chair—rope tied tight around his wrists and ankles. A hazy light came from the circular hole above him.

"You wish to leave?"

The voice echoed throughout the pit. Then there were footsteps behind him. Getting louder.

And louder.

Jacob passed by the chair so close that he almost bumped into it. He turned to Ike, his face expressionless and distorted in the smoke. A cigarette rested between his lips. The end glowed orange.

Ike had never seen Jacob smoke before. As far as Ike knew, no one was allowed to smoke or drink at the campsite. "One must not pollute the body," Jacob told the congregation often.

"What are you doing?" Ike asked, his voice wobbling with fear.

"I've seen a new vision, Icarus. One that involves a sacrifice—"

"I want my clothes!" Ike yelled, pulling and twisting at the ropes.

"The Divine Path will be consumed in a wall of flame, and I will be betrayed as Christ was by Judas," Jacob continued with steady, calm words. "But you . . . you and your friends will survive. For five years. The rest of us need time—time to prepare for the new world."

With this, Jacob stepped back and disappeared in the smoke. Ike strained to see the orange glow of his cigarette, but that, too, was gone.

"Let me go!"

Ike yanked his right arm. The rope slipped somewhat, but it only seemed to cut into his skin. Then he pushed his feet hard against the floor, trying to knock the chair over. But it wouldn't move. His throat was burning from the smoke, and Ike could feel tears streaming down his cheeks.

"Smoking is bad for you!" Ike screamed. He wanted to say something hurtful, but that was the only thing he could think of through the fear and the anger and the humiliation of being naked.

Jacob chuckled directly behind Ike.

"You're right," Jacob said, his lips inches from Ike's ears, his breath hot and moist. "I should put this out."

Suddenly Jacob pressed the glowing end of the cigarette into Ike's left forearm. Ike writhed and screamed.

"No!" Ike cried. *"Please . . . stop!"*

Jacob used his other hand to hold Ike's arm in place. The smell of burning flesh filled Ike's nose.

"You tried to fly away, Icarus. On wings of wax . . . ," Jacob intoned as he blew on the tip of the cigarette. Ike watched it glow bright orange again. "This is what happens when you don't listen."

The cigarette burned a new place on his arm, and Ike screamed until his voice went hoarse. . . .

Yes, Allison remembers the story. She remembers Ike's nightmares after that day too. He'd yell in his sleep or start moaning real loud, and when he woke up, all he could remember was being burned alive. Sometimes he was trapped in a house fire or a burning building. Other times he was being held over the flames of a campfire.

It frightened Allison to see how much Ike changed after that trip to the Confessional. A week earlier he had given her the orange yellow dreamcatcher. "I made this for you," he said, his smile bright as the sunlight. How he'd found time to make it and where he'd gotten the string, she never knew. But she knew it made her feel special. Sure, she didn't *like* him like him, but it was nice to feel the heat of someone's crush. To think that she could make someone's heart beat faster.

That was special.

But Ike's face and eyes never looked the same after Jacob burned him. They were distant, shaky.

And now Ike looks back at Allison with those same tortured eyes.

"Emma's room smelled that way this morning, you know.

Like burned skin," Ike says, swallowing hard. "When I was standing there looking at her, all I could think of was myself. I was more afraid for *me* than I was sad for Emma. Can you believe that?" Ike lowers his head.

"We're all scared," Allison says, and then she realizes this might be her problem too. It's not that Emma was practically a stranger that bothers Allison so much. It's that she wants to *feel* something more for her. All her sadness is mixed with terrible memories and uncertainty. It's mixed with fear, and fear just makes you selfish.

Emma deserves more, Allison admits. A lot more.

"Hey," David calls out as he and Jade step into the lobby.

David is wearing the same jeans and black T-shirt from yesterday. In fact, everyone is wearing the same clothes except Jade. She must have changed before following them to Emma's room. Her short red skirt sparkles with shiny beads, and her black lacy top is almost see-through.

Sheriff Cooper watches for a moment from the doorway before speaking. "Y'all need to stay around for the next few days. You're material witnesses to this crime, and we'll have more questions that need answering. Understand?"

Sheriff Cooper doesn't wait for them to answer. He just hooks his thumbs into his belt and turns slightly when another officer enters the room. This man is tall like David, except with blond hair and blue eyes. He doesn't look much older than seventeen himself.

"This is Deputy Archibald," the sheriff announces. "He's going to take you"—he points to Jade—"and Ike back to the hotel. I'll drive you two," he says, looking at David and Allison.

"Just give me a minute," Sheriff Cooper adds before leaving the room. His footsteps sound heavy and labored as he walks down the hall.

Deputy Archibald opens the front door quickly. "Come on.

Let's go," he says, his voice high and thin like a tightrope.

Jade mutters, "Later," over her shoulder, and Ike quickly follows her through the doorway.

David stands close to Allison now. This is the first time that they've been alone since she got back to Meridian. It is what she has wanted. To be alone with him. To be close to him. But now she doesn't know what to say.

"I need to know something, Allison." David's words break the silence. "The truth, okay?"

Allison nods.

"Who's next?"

"What?"

"In your dreams, which one of us dies next?"

Allison can't believe the question.

It feels as if someone has just kicked her in the stomach and knocked the air right out of her. She looks at David, wishing that her heart didn't change rhythm every time she noticed the sadness in his eyes.

"I . . . I have no idea." The words stumble from her mouth as she steps away.

"What's wrong?" David asks.

"*What's wrong?*" Allison snaps. "What kind of person do you think I am?"

"I—"

"Don't you think that I would have done something if I knew Emma was going to die? Don't you think I would have warned her? Or Harold?"

David lowers his eyes, sorry.

"I didn't mean it that way," he says sheepishly. "I thought you might be trying to protect us, you know? Trying not to freak us out or something."

"No," she mutters. But really, she wants to shake him. She wants to be able to say: "Don't you know *me* well enough?"

But of course, he doesn't. How could he? And this makes her feel hurt all over again.

Before Allison can say anything at all, Sheriff Cooper enters from the hall door. "Y'all ready?"

"Definitely," Allison says fast, without even glancing at David.

Like Jade, she barrels out of the station, not looking over her shoulder to see Sheriff Cooper or David. Right then she misses her car. The freedom to hit the road. To go anywhere. To get as far away as possible.

8

TALKING WITHOUT WORDS

Jade's suitcase is on her bed and mostly packed when David and Allison get there. The hotel's cheap furniture and hideously ugly bedspread aren't amusing now. They're just cheap and hideously ugly. Emma's room was identical to Jade's, and Allison has to work hard not to picture Emma's body on the bed. Her white skin and missing eyes. The horrible smell—

Allison stops. She wants to sit but can't bring herself to use the puffy chair that Emma was on yesterday. It wouldn't feel right, she thinks. It just wouldn't. Instead she stands by the end table. Across from her, Ike leans against the wall, watching Jade pack.

"You sure you have to leave so soon?" he asks.

Jade steps out of the bathroom and shoves a small toiletries bag into the suitcase. "No, I thought I'd hang around until someone burns my eyes out."

"The sheriff told us we have to stay for a while," David says earnestly. He lingers by the open door.

"Well, he can drive his fat ass up to D.C. and arrest me." Jade closes the suitcase and sits on the bed. Like everyone else, she avoids the puffy chair as if Emma were still sitting in it.

"Maybe Jade's right. Why don't we just get out of here?" Ike asks.

"*Thank you,*" Jade replies.

"Do whatever you want, Ike," Allison says more harshly than she expected. She wonders if Ike and Jade think the same thing that David does, the same thing that Jacob did all those years ago. That Allison can see the future in her dreams. "We can't just go home and pretend none of this ever happened. We all know what this could mean. . . ."

"What?" Ike pushes.

Allison expects Jade to chime in with her trademark rudeness, but instead she is quiet. Her body is still, except for her fingers. They start dancing quietly on her thighs. Some hovering in the air, others pressing into the skin. Jade must be playing some piece of music, Allison thinks. But that's not all. There is something oddly beautiful and sad about those fingers with the blue nail polish. The way they move and stay slightly curved. Any boy could fall in love with her hands, Allison admits.

"Well?" Ike insists. "What could it mean?"

Allison looks up at him. "That Jacob's prophecy is coming true."

Finally, Allison says to herself. *Someone said it.* Ike's fear. Jade's attitude. David's hurtful question. Even her own dreams. They're all about the same thing. They're afraid Jacob might be right.

"But what if someone is doing this to make it *seem* that way? I mean . . . what if someone else survived the fire that night? One of the adults," David says thoughtfully, and Allison can tell that he isn't looking for a fight. He has been listening to her. Really listening, she realizes. In a way that no one else ever has. He treats her words and ideas with respect.

She considers his question while wishing that he weren't standing so far away, his loose body leaning against the doorframe. "You mean, to convince the people that Jacob's prophecies are coming true?" she asks. "To revive the cult?"

"I'm still not hearing a good reason to stick around," Ike says.

"Emma." The word slips out of Allison's mouth, and Ike tucks his hands in his pockets.

"Look," Allison continues. "We can't let Jacob's cult start up again, Ike. You remember the things he did. We can't let that happen to anyone else."

With those words Jade's fingers stop moving.

"You can't be fucking serious," she snaps as she stands up and holds out her hands for everyone to see, her fingers spread apart. Most of them are crooked and twisted, and they remind Allison of the old map in her history teacher's class. The parchment cracked and yellow with age. Its texture sturdy and fragile.

"Nothing supernatural did this," Jade continues, her eyes fierce. "Jacob did. Jacob cut Allison's neck. He burned Ike's arm. He almost drowned Harold several times. That's torture, not the hand of God. And the world isn't going to end just because some crazy man said so five years ago!"

Jade reaches for her suitcase again. As she puts her hands against it, she stops for a second. Staring at them.

"I still play, you know. I might even go to a conservatory one day," she says quietly. "They can't move as fast, and they hurt when it gets cold out. But I'll never stop playing. I won't let Jacob take that away from me. . . ."

The upright piano in the main hall was the perfect instrument for the end of the world. Dusty and old and falling apart. Many of the plastic keys were cracked or melted with cigarette burns. A few at the top didn't make any sound at all when Jade pushed on them, but she didn't really mind.

You hardly play up there anyway, she told herself.

As far as being in tune . . . well, it wasn't even close. It could still be played, though. You just had to get used to it. Jade always figured the instrument had its own language that way, and that she'd learned it so well that most folks thought she was a native speaker.

The piano made her special at the compound, Jade

explained to them. Everyone got real quiet when she played. Grown-ups talked about her after supper. And old Mrs. Haggerty often took her aside to lament the day she stopped taking lessons.

"My mother always told me I'd regret it," old Mrs. Haggerty said with her wobbly voice.

Blah, blah, blah . . .

There might not have been any music teachers at camp, but Jade wasn't going to stop playing anytime soon. That was for damn sure. This was one thing she could do better than anybody else there. Even Jacob.

And Jade liked it that way.

Her parents did too. They were never much in the talking department. Her father, Bruce Rowan, preferred grunting as his primary means of communication before the days of the Divine Path. While Mrs. R. smiled so often you had no idea what she was thinking. But both of them listened to Jade with a *look, that's my daughter* expression on their faces—especially when the congregation gathered around.

Although being prideful was probably a sin (though Jacob never really talked about that), Jade could tell they were proud. Her father would cross his arms in front of his chest and lean back in a way that made him look like someone who'd just finished eating an enormous meal. Her mother . . . well, she smiled, of course.

And on the days that something deep in Jade's chest hurts from missing her parents, she's glad to know she made them happy at least a few times in her life.

Jacob allowed her to practice every afternoon in preparation for Sunday service. Soon this became Jade's favorite part of the day. For thirty minutes it was just she and the music.

Almost everything else at the camp involved other people—sleeping in one-room cabins, sharing meals, going to classes, praying. Even the crappers, the outdoor toilets that the grown-ups called privies, were crowded with folks. No, you never had a minute for yourself, Jade remembers. No time to think. To be on your own. To dream about the days before the Divine Path.

Except at the piano.

Jade was practicing Brahms the day Jacob visited. The thick, C major chords of the intermezzo filled the empty hall. They were bright and energetic, but with a touch of sadness, like seeing gray clouds on a sunny day.

She wasn't used to anyone coming around during practice, so Jacob's voice startled her. It made her heart accelerate and her jaw tense. Still, without thinking, Jade kept her hands on the keyboard right where she left off, the way some people use bookmarks when they read.

"I want to speak with you," Jacob said, his voice clashing with the beauty of the notes still hanging in the air.

"Yes, Jacob."

He leaned against the piano, looking down at her. His eyes were yellow, though her mother called them hazel, and his chin came out to a point, making his entire face look like a crescent moon.

"It is about your faith." Jacob paused, and Jade could smell the sweat of his body. It reminded her of hard-boiled eggs. "Recently your voice has been silent during prayer. You don't call out with the others in praise. You don't seem moved by his Word."

Jacob reached down and pressed one of the keys that made no sound.

"Your mind is elsewhere, Jade . . . but not when you play." Jacob lifted his eyebrows and waited in the way that grown-ups wait when they want you to spill the beans about something.

Jade remained silent. Unreadable. She'd learned that from her father.

"Faith is not a gift," Jacob continued. "It is something you must work at. Like playing Schubert's music."

"Brahms," Jade corrected.

"Excuse me?"

"It's Brahms, not Schubert," Jade said, keeping her voice flat and even.

The half smile on Jacob's face faded, and he stepped away from the piano. "It would be tragic to lose your faith *and* your ability to play, don't you think?"

Jade nodded, and without another word he left.

After that Jacob prevented her from getting anywhere near the piano. New chores filled the late afternoon—sweeping floors, setting possum traps, gathering firewood for the kitchen, and helping David and Ike take garbage to the compost heap.

Jade wasn't asked to play for Sunday services, either. Mr. Jenkins, who could hardly see a thing with or without his glasses, pounded out some hymns, and the congregation sang along. No one seemed to care that he knew only three songs. Worse than that, no one seemed to miss Jade's playing.

At least, no one said anything to her.

Even her mother didn't appear troubled by the change—until Jade complained that it wasn't fair, that she still had faith but didn't want to be a damn phony about it.

Slap.

It was the first time her mother hit her.

The shock hurt more than her open palm. Her mother had always been gentle as silk.

"We are doing something far more important here," she told her daughter, without a smile or a hint of compassion. "Don't ruin it with your selfishness and complaints."

She shuffled off to evening prayers, and her footsteps kicked up hardly any dust. That was the first time Jade understood the power that Jacob had to change people.

The next day Jade went by the main hall around the time

she used to practice. She thought Mr. Jenkins might be there, refining the art of wrong notes and crappy playing, but not a single sound came from inside. A lock was on the door.

What the hell?

Jade had obeyed Jacob. She did her lousy chores and put off doing the one thing that made her happy. But she hadn't seen this before. None of the other doors on the compound were locked. Everything was open, even Jacob's cabin.

Something about the lock lit a fire deep inside her. She dropped the garbage pail in her hand and hurried around the side of the building. The window on the back left was always stuck halfway between open and closed, and she knew she could squeeze through.

The interior of the hall felt cool, and Jade wiped the sweat from her forehead.

There it was. The piano. Dusty and old and falling apart as always. But it looked different to her now. It was the thing that Jacob had tried to take away from her because . . . because music was more important to Jade than Jacob, the Divine Path, or anything else.

It had become her religion.

She touched the keys, and her fingers came to life. She played the loudest, fastest pieces she could. Beethoven. Brahms. Chopin. Big chords that made the entire piano shake with beautiful fury.

Anything but Schubert, she thought with a smile, and closed her eyes to listen. . . .

The lock and chain rattled before the door of the main hall swung open. Jade looked over her shoulder and saw the Doctor standing there. He didn't move. He just motioned to her in the way he always did when it was time to go to the Confessional.

Jade didn't care, though. She closed the lid with the same

care Jacob gave to the Good Book after a sermon. Then she marched right out of the hall and toward the Confessional. She wasn't going to let the Doctor take her there. She wasn't going to let him or Jacob think that she was afraid.

Hell no.

Inside, the Confessional was thick with smoke. The mirrors made the room feel enormous and claustrophobic at the same time. With each step your own reflections seemed to push in around you. Crowding and watchful.

"Hello?" Jade called out as she walked toward the pit.

Her voice echoed below and faded quickly. There were no other sounds. No birds or cicadas singing outside. No hint of the gurgling stream in the nearby ravine. Only the late-afternoon darkness seeped through the walls.

Then Jade heard something sizzle beneath her, like water being poured on hot coals. The smoke billowed up more heavily now. She leaned over the edge for a better look.

Slowly.

Her eyes were stinging from the smokiness when—

A hand latched on to her ankle. It yanked her forward in one violent motion. She tumbled headfirst into the pit. . . .

Jade's head throbbed when she finally opened her eyes. She must have hit the ground hard. The rotten taste of dirt filled her mouth.

She tried to touch her face but couldn't move. Her arms were trapped—buried inside the dirt wall in front of her. She tried pulling them out, but they wouldn't budge. Not an inch. The holes were deep and not much wider than her arms. The muddy soil pressed against her skin.

She couldn't get any leverage to pull away, either. She was on her knees, her chest and the right side of her face against the wall.

Jade wanted to scream and to cry at the same time, but she

was too afraid at first—afraid of drawing attention to herself. She tried pulling away again and realized that her hands were free and uncovered on the other side of the wall. Something cold and metallic was fastened around each wrist, though. Handcuffs or chains of some kind, she figured.

That's when she first heard the sound behind her. Steady, nasal breathing. Someone was watching her, but she couldn't turn her head far enough to see.

"Jacob?" she mumbled.

The sounds stopped for a moment, then continued. This time she could hear feet sliding in the dirt as well. He was moving away from her now. Into another room, it seemed. With one ear pressed against the wall, though, Jade couldn't make out the faraway sounds. She tried to yank her arms free in one big motion.

Nothing.

The struggle only made her feel more trapped.

An icy coldness suddenly touched her hands.

She screamed.

The cold pressed against her fingers and wrists, prodding at first. Someone was trying to grab them . . . trying to hold her still. Jade could feel the tears streaming down her cheeks and chin as she shook her hands. Her mouth still tasted of dirt and smoke.

The strong, icy grip on the other side finally tightened around her right hand. Two hands wrapped around one. Enveloping. Suffocating.

A few seconds passed and nothing happened. Enough time for her to get still, to breathe more easily, to wonder what was happening. Until—

Snap.

Her index finger shattered.

Jade screamed so loud she thought her throat was on fire. She pulled and squirmed and yelled: *"No!"*

But the grip on her right hand didn't loosen. He moved to her next finger.

Snap.

Each finger. One at a time.

The bones breaking.

Snap.

Snap.

Not the thumb. Just the fingers.

It stopped. A few seconds passed, and she could feel warm urine spilling down her legs. Her screams had become sobs. Everything became still.

Then the man on the other side of the wall started on her left hand. . . .

Before that day Jade had preferred to talk without words. Maybe she got it from her father. Except she used a piano instead of grunts and disapproving stares. But after that Jade spoke with her voice more, not less. She didn't give Jacob any reason to question her belief. She called out the loudest "Amen's" and "Hallelujah's" at services.

Not from faith. But from anger. From the hope that the force of her unbelieving words would pummel him.

Long after her fingers healed—healed as well as they could—she continued to use words like fists. To lash out first. To keep her distance. That way, she figured, no one could know what you really cared about.

That way, no one could take it away.

"Some*one* is trying to kill us," Jade says coolly as she lifts her suitcase off the bed. "Maybe you're right, Allison. Maybe it's about reviving Jacob's cult and convincing people that the world is about to end. I don't know."

Jade steps past Ike and David and pauses at the door. "But I don't really give a fuck. I'm going home."

"What about Harold and Emma? Don't we owe them . . .

something?" Allison asks, struggling to find the right words, the right reasons.

"Like what? A higher body count?" Jade looks at Ike, but he doesn't respond. "Don't you get it?" she asks all of them. "This is it. This is our chance to get out of here for good. To leave all of this shit behind. The town. The memories—"

"Five years," David says, with his eyes lowered and his shoulders curled forward. "It's been five years, and I haven't forgotten a thing. I mean . . . we killed a man. I know we had to, but . . ." He pauses, looking up. His eyes are watery and distant. "How are we supposed to get over that?"

"Well, hanging around here isn't going to help," Jade says.

"Okay, forget about Harold and Emma." Allison turns to Jade, though she is still thinking about David's words. How true they are. How many times she's wished she could wipe away her past like words on a chalkboard. To erase the guilt and the fear. "Forget about the cult and what it did to us. What about you?"

"What about me?"

"You think you're safe? You think that whatever is doing this won't come after you? That it won't find you?"

Jade adjusts her grip on the suitcase. "I prefer to be a moving target."

"None of us are safe," Allison continues. "Not until we stop what's happening."

Jade exhales but doesn't move.

"Look," Allison presses, and her voice cracks slightly. "Let's find out the truth about what happened. Let's end this."

"How?" Ike blurts out. He has been watching the conversation like someone at a tennis match, and now he shifts uneasily from one foot to the other.

Allison walks across the room to her bag. "I want to talk to this guy," she says, pulling out the newspaper article about

Harold's death and handing it to Ike. The name Marcum Shale is circled at the top.

"I Googled him," Allison explains. "He works at the Meridian Public Library. He might know something about Harold—about why he came back here."

"And if he doesn't?" Ike asks, concentrating on the paper.

Before Allison can answer, a whistling wind starts to push its way through the door, and it howls like a lonesome dog looking at the moon. She waits for it to quiet down.

"I'm not sure." Allison shrugs. "At least it's a start."

"Well, that all sounds like a blast," Jade says as she opens the door. "But no thanks. I'm outta here."

Jade hesitates, and as she looks around at everyone, Allison sees something sad cross her face, something genuine.

"It's been real," Jade says quickly. "Later."

With that, the expression is gone.

And so is Jade.

9

NUMBERS

The Meridian Public Library is connected to the town hall, which is nothing more than a one-room building with wood floors and a portrait of George W. Bush on the south wall. The library building gets used for everything from school bake sales to hoedowns for retired folks. The library itself is L shaped, wrapping around two sides of the town hall. The longer side is almost entirely filled with books about the Civil War. Mr. Beederman, the librarian for more than thirty years, considers the War of Northern Aggression the only real war worth reading about in U.S. history. He also thinks "Yankee" is just about the worst thing you can call a person—that and "liberal."

Since Meridian Elementary doesn't have a library of its own, every kid in every grade has to go to Beederman's Book Barn at some point. That's what most folks call it—the Barn, for short, since the library was originally a stable and it still smells like hay.

The Barn hasn't changed much in five years, Allison observes. The circulation desk is still no bigger than her desk at the Packer house, though it's a lot cleaner, and a faded poster hangs on the wall by the door. Yellow letters at the top spell out the word READ. The rest shows an open book with a pair of glasses on top.

The glasses remind her of Emma.

Emma would have felt right at home here, Allison thinks. Sitting behind the desk and helping folks find books on the neatly ordered shelves. She turns to David and Ike to say something, to see if they might be thinking the same, but they aren't looking at her. They seem lost in their own memories.

"Can I help you?" a young woman with shoulder-length brown hair asks. She sits behind the desk with a book in her lap, and the badge on her lapel reads: LINDA, VOLUNTEER.

"Yes," Allison says. "We're looking for Marcum Shale."

"Mr. Marcum?" Linda asks, closing her book. "He doesn't come in on the weekends. But he'll be here bright and early Monday morning."

Allison hesitates, unsure of what to say. "We might not be around then. You see, we're just visiting. . . . We grew up here."

"Oh," she says, glancing at Ike and David with a smile. "I knew I didn't recognize y'all. I'm kinda new here myself. About three months now, since my grandma got sick. I'm from Tallahassee. Well, I still am. I'm just here helping Gran for a while." She pauses. "So, you knew Mr. Marcum a while back, then?"

Allison nods. "Yeah."

"We didn't want to leave without saying hi," Ike says as he steps up to the desk, and Allison is relieved for the help.

"I could try calling him," Linda says, opening the top drawer of the desk and shuffling through some papers. "I don't see a number here. Maybe it's in the back office." She looks up and chuckles. "Well, it's more like a storeroom."

"A storeroom?" Ike echoes, running his hand through his hair, and Allison suddenly wonders if he's flirting with Linda the Volunteer.

"Yeah, I can show you, if you'd like. It's where Mr. Marcum keeps all the town records—birth certificates, news-paper articles, census reports, things like that." Linda stands up from the desk. "Yeah," she continues. "He's got file cabinets filled with stuff. He's quite the collector, you know."

She leads them around the corner, past the stacks of Civil War books. The corridor seems to get narrower with each step, as if the building is coming to a point, and they have to follow her in a single-file line. Ike stays closest to Linda, then Allison and David. There are no windows here, just metal shelves and fluorescent lights overhead. The library is empty except for them.

Linda steps into the last aisle and pauses in front of a door. It is in the farthest-away, darkest place in the building.

"Let's see," she mutters, opening the door with a brass key and snapping on the light switch by the entry.

A single bulb buzzes overhead, giving off more noise than light. The low ceiling curves slightly downward, and as they step inside, David has to duck his head. The room is narrow and much longer than Allison expected. Newspapers and books are stacked precariously against every inch of the walls.

It smells strongly of horses.

Linda walks across the room and starts leafing through some papers on the desk. "It should be here," she says.

Dozens of yellow pads are piled on top of one another, and they seem to be filled with handwritten notes. At one corner a space has been cleared for a framed black-and-white picture. But it's too faded to make out.

Two steel-gray file cabinets lean against the back wall. On top of one there is an old, metallic fan that doesn't look like it has worked since 1865. More newspapers are piled on top of one another.

"I keep telling Mr. Marcum that he should straighten things up a bit. How he can find anything in this mess is beyond me," Linda says, still looking through the papers. "I'm sorry. I'm just not seeing anything. . . ."

"Maybe it's out front somewhere?" Ike suggests, his voice rough like bark yet sincere. It reminds Allison of the way men talk to women in movies, not real life.

"Well . . . it could be on the new schedule," Linda says as she puts her hands on her hips. "We can run back over there and check—"

"I can come with you," Ike offers, and he moves toward the door before she can answer. "Allison hasn't been feeling well all day. It'd be better if she could stay here and rest a bit."

"Well . . . ," Linda starts.

"I'd really appreciate it," Allison says in her trying-to-sound-sick voice.

"We'll be along in a few minutes," David adds.

After hesitating for a moment, Linda nods, then she leaves with Ike right behind her.

Even though Allison figures that Ike is trying to give them some time to snoop around the office, she can tell that he *is* flirting with Linda too. Part of her wants to remind him that Jade left only ten minutes ago. Of course, it didn't take Allison long to put Bo on the back burner when she first saw David. For Ike, it might be his overcharged hormones that have him following Linda back into the hall like a puppy dog.

Or maybe he has a rubber-band heart. Flexible enough for anyone at any time. Flexible enough to snap right back into place after being stretched out and let go. But not Allison. Her heart has always felt like a fruit that bruises too easily. Sure, she doesn't love Bo, but she has never pretended to. She also doesn't know what she's feeling for David. Whether or not it's love, she wonders how much more bruising she can take.

As soon as Linda and Ike are out of sight, David steps over to the file cabinet and opens the top drawer.

"What are you looking for?" Allison asks.

"The library lady said that Marcum keeps town records," David says over his shoulder. "There's gotta be something here about Jacob, right?"

As David flips through the first few files, Allison starts

looking through the other cabinet. Being this close to him makes her think of Bo again. Those nights behind the coffee shop. Kissing instead of talking. His fingertips running along the scar. That would make things a lot easier right now, Allison thinks. If she could just kiss David and they didn't have to talk at all.

She glances over at him. His long, strong fingers shuffle through several folders, and she wishes he would hold her hand again. Just for a second. Then, all of a sudden, he turns to her with a quick smile.

Her heart flutters.

David returns to the manila folders beneath his fingers, and she does the same. They don't have much time before Linda and Ike get back.

All of the cabinet drawers seem to be organized by date: 2000–2001, 2002–3, 2004–5. . . . Allison focuses on 2002–3.

"Allison?" David asks. This time he doesn't look at her.

"Yeah?"

"I'm sorry about earlier."

Her heart flutters again.

"Me too."

At the back of the drawer she finds a file marked JULY 2002. The file feels heavy in her hands, and the outside is more soiled than the others. Dozens of newspaper articles crowd the front. Papers from all over the country—*New York Times, San Francisco Chronicle, Raleigh News and Observer, Denver Post*. . . . All of them feature stories about the fire that killed Jacob Crawley and the adult members of the Divine Path. Several include a grainy picture of him—his silver white hair and a smile that could hide the greatest sins.

Allison has never seen any news coverage on the cult. She never wanted to. But she can't believe all of this. Somehow it doesn't seem real that the whole country was reading about *them*. To her, the world seemed a lot smaller then. Meridian. Daddy. Mel. Jacob. Her friends. That was pretty much it. But these newspapers make what Jacob was doing bigger somehow, she thinks.

Bigger and more frightening.

"Look at this," Allison says to David, handing him a few of the clippings.

He stands closer to her now, and she can breathe him in. His smell reminds her of Mr. Packer's garden. Fresh soil and leafy plants. As he reads, she continues looking through the folder. There is a faint wheezing sound every time he exhales.

The next sheet of paper in the file is burned slightly at one end, and she wonders if it was salvaged from the fire. The handwritten text is discolored and somewhat smudged:

And round about the throne were four and twenty seats: and upon the seats I saw four and twenty elders sitting, clothed in white raiment; and they had on their heads crowns of gold.

It was Jacob's prophecy about the end time and the new world to come, she remembers. He often read to the congregation from the book of Revelation, but this was one of the few passages that he asked his followers to know from the heart. It was the passage they recited before Jacob preached for the last time.

His final words, his final two promises, have stayed with Allison like handprints dried in cement. Permanent. Hard. She can picture Jacob that day. He wore the same white linen suit he always wore, even though the air was so thick and humid that you practically had to swim through it. Sweat drenched his body, and his yellow eyes flickered like candlelight.

It was three days before the fire.

"I have seen the end, brothers and sisters. I have seen it in my dreams and in the visions of our children—visions that are still pure and uncorrupted by too many years on this earth." He gestured to Allison and David and Ike and Jade and Emma and Harold. They sat in the front row, as always.

"In five years' time God will destroy the earth and all its wickedness with fire. But there will be no ark. No Noah. No animals carried to safety.

"Not this time.

"This time it must all be destroyed. It must burn for the Lord to begin again with a new garden and a new paradise. It must burn so the Chosen can be reborn as rulers and law-makers.

"The revelation of the Lord tells us that twenty-four elders will reign over the kingdoms of the earth. And I tell you once again that we are the twenty-four. We are the Chosen who will rise up from the ashes to govern the new world with justice and wisdom, with vengeance and mercy.

"Praise be, I say.

"Praise be."

Even back then Allison understood that Jacob never promised salvation. He only promised power. He promised the grown-ups that they would rule the earth. That they would have the kind of power that they had never felt in their own lives. The power not to be fired from a job or to be left by a wife or husband. The power to see the good rewarded and the wicked punished. The power to start over.

And who doesn't want that every once in a while? Allison thinks.

Her Daddy even promised her that men like the one who killed Mel would be punished in the next world. An idea that didn't sound bad at all, Allison remembers.

What sounded bad was saying good-bye. That's the second thing Jacob promised:

"The Divine Path will be consumed in a wall of flame, for we, too, must be cleansed. As we prepare for the new world, our children, the Visionaries, will stay behind. They will wait until the Lord is ready to reunite us, until he takes their lives on this earth as a sign that the end is here.

"Do not be afraid.

"Do not shed any tears.

"It is his will."

"Whose will?" Allison wanted to scream. Jacob was asking her to say good-bye to Daddy, and that was the last straw. She had said good-bye too many times in her life. Not again.

Something had to be done. She had to stop him.

"They got it wrong," David says, and Allison looks up from the folder in her hands. "All of them."

"What?"

"Look here." He points to a line and reads: "'A fire in Meridian, North Carolina claimed the lives of twenty-three people yesterday, all of whom were members of a cult known as the Divine Path.'"

"Twenty-three?"

"Yeah, they all say twenty-three."

"But that would mean . . ." Allison stops, still staring at the papers in David's hands. Twenty-four adults. Six children. Those were prophetic numbers for Jacob. Something he talked about often. Something that only cult members would know about.

"Someone else *did* survive the fire," David says with a whisper.

Allison's mind starts to race. Someone—not some *thing*, not the power of some prophecy—must be chasing them. But how? She still can't explain what happened to Emma and Harold.

Before she can say anything else to David, Linda calls out across the room. The shrill sound of her voice makes Allison jump.

"What's going on here?" Linda says more as an accusation than a question. "I don't think you should be touching Mr. Marcum's things."

She hurries toward them and takes the folder from Allison's hands. "He's very particular." Linda shakes her head the way parents do when they want to make you feel bad and guilty at the same time. She then grabs the clippings from David, shoves them inside the file, and presses it against her chest. "Very particular."

"Sorry," David mutters, his eyes lowered.

"Yeah," Allison adds. "We didn't mean to upset you."

"Not me," Linda corrects. "Mr. Marcum."

"He seems really interested in the Divine Path," David says in a pleasant, almost casual tone.

Linda nods.

"So many clippings," David adds.

"Well, he's not the only one," Linda begins tentatively. "Lots of folks have been talking about Jacob again. Mr. Marcum. Sheriff Cooper. Smiley Peters. Jennifer—"

"Talking how?" Allison blurts out.

Linda's body stiffens a bit. "Not the way you might think."

"I'm surprised anyone is talking at all," David says coaxingly. "It seems like ancient history to me."

Linda leans forward, and Allison can tell that this woman enjoys telling secrets. A thin smile brightens her face.

"Oh, they're talking, all right," Linda continues. "But not like you might think. Not about him being crazy. It's just the opposite. They talk like Jacob was this great man or something. They say he saw the future—"

"Wait a minute," Allison interrupts again. "Where's Ike?"

"What?"

"Ike." Allison's voice tightens. "Where is he?"

"He said he'd wait for you outside. I guess he was feeling a bit claustrophobic. Some folks don't take well to bein' in quiet places."

"He left?"

"Why, yes." Linda's eyebrows furrow, and she gestures toward the door. "I think it's time you leave too . . ."

But before she can finish, Allison rushes out of the office and into the long corridor of books. It doesn't make sense, she thinks. Ike "I Think It's Better to Travel in Packs" Dempsey wouldn't leave. Not even to try his cell phone again or to step out for some air or to knock back a shot of tequila.

No way.

She can hear David closing in behind her, their footsteps slapping loudly against the floor. As she turns the corner, Allison almost knocks over a small table with library flyers. She was hoping to see Ike in the lobby, with a smirk on his face and his orange hair sticking up as if his whole body were charged with static. But he's not here. The lobby is empty. Only the poster of eyeglasses without eyes looks back at her.

Something is wrong, Allison says to herself. She can feel it in her somersaulting stomach as she pushes open the front door.

The white light outside is blinding. She squints, but it doesn't seem to help. The brightness only seems to get worse.

Suddenly her legs buckle. Allison can feel herself falling down. Falling into a hard, burning light . . .

White light reflects off a silver blade. It is long, with jagged edges. Silver teeth. Hungry and savage.

They bite down hard, and red blood spills out of the white skin. The jagged blade stops, stuck against the bone. It starts again.

Back and forth . . .

Back and forth . . .

The girl's hands are bound to a steering wheel, tight. She tries to pull free. Her mouth open, screaming without sound. Only soft piano music can be heard in the distance.

Rain starts to fall, but it is not cool. The thick, heavy drops coat the windshield red until the girl disappears from view. . . .

10

TAKING PICTURES

"Allison?"

David's voice seems far away, but when her eyes come into focus and the whiteness fades, she can see him kneeling by her side. Her legs feel stiff and rubbery, her throat dry. Everything around her—David's face, the library door, her car parked on the street—is blurry, as if she were watching an out-of-focus film.

As David helps her to her feet, she notices the medication bottle in his hand.

"I found this in your pocket," he says.

She twists off the cap and puts a pill in her mouth. It tastes bitter on her tongue. "Thanks."

"Maybe you should see a doctor," David says as he takes the cell phone from his back pocket and presses some buttons. "Damn . . . I still can't get a signal. . . ."

"It's okay. I'm fine," Allison mutters, trying to ignore her throbbing headache and the fear of what's happening to her. The seizures. The visions. It's all getting worse, she thinks. "Really."

"No, you're not fine," David snaps. "You're not even close to fine. You're, like, the opposite of fine." He pauses. "We need to get you to a hospital."

"We don't have time for that," Allison says, her head spinning like water down a drain. "I saw something . . . Jade, I think. Tied up in her car. I think she's still in town. I—where's Ike?"

"I don't know. He wasn't out here when you fell."

"Crap." Allison tries to hurry to her car but stops at the rear bumper. Her legs shake unsteadily. She is out of breath. "I can't drive."

"No kidding," David mutters.

"Look, we need to find them."

"*How*, Allison?" David asks angrily. There is a hard quality to his face. "Jade's gone. Ike's gone. And if you keep passing out on the street . . . well, I don't even know what. We need a doctor."

"There's nothing a doctor can tell me that I don't already know. I have epilepsy. Period."

David recoils slightly. "That . . . that doesn't mean we can't do something—"

"There's no cure, David. There's no changing it. So all I can do is take my pills and hope for the best. Most of the time they keep me from having seizures—"

"Most of the time?"

"*Yes*, most of the time." She leans against the trunk for support. "Maybe something about this place is making them worse. I don't know. But right now you have to trust me, okay? I can handle it."

Without waiting for him to respond, Allison reaches into her pocket and pulls out her car keys. "Maybe Ike went back to the hotel to wait for us."

David takes the keys reluctantly. His face seems heavy—heavy with exhaustion and fear and doubt. Allison can tell that he doesn't believe for one second that Ike is safe. She doesn't either.

Inside the car Allison leans back in the seat. Her body aches, and her head still pounds. The hum and vibrations of the engine are soothing. It's strange being in the passenger seat of her car, though. It feels familiar and different at the same time, like trying on your best friend's clothes.

"I've never let anyone drive my car before," Allison says. "It's weird."

"I'll try not to crash, then."

"Funny." She glances at him, and there is a smirk on his face.

As they leave town, the trees get thicker. Allison closes her eyes, and the pounding of her head seems to lessen. The tires thump along the uneven road. The wind whistles through the poorly insulated windows.

"Talk," she says.

"Talk?"

"Yeah."

"About what?"

"Anything," she tells him. "I just want to hear the sound of your voice."

After a moment, David starts talking.

"Cameras. I have lots of them: a couple of Nikon digital SLRs, some old Nikon film cameras with everything from a fish-eye lens to a four-hundred-millimeter telephoto like the ones that sports photographers use. I even have a medium format Hasselblad. But my favorite is the Leica M3 with a simple fifty-millimeter lens."

"Sounds complicated to me," Allison replies.

"It was my dad's," David continues. "He loved taking pictures—before we moved to Meridian, that is. Photography was his favorite thing next to falling asleep on the couch and watching Jimmy Stewart films.

"'Who's that?' I'd ask, as if Dad hadn't forced me to watch *It's a Wonderful Life* a thousand times.

"'The last great actor,' he'd say with the same tone he'd begin his most-repeated sentence of all time: 'Back in my day . . .' Then fill in the blank with whatever you just did wrong. 'Back in my day we had manners.' 'Back in my day we respected our elders.' 'Back in my day we cared about getting good grades.'. . .

"But I figure Grandpa dished out a whole bunch of 'Back-in-my-day's' too, and Dad was simply carrying on the family tradition.

"Mom preferred Sean Connery to Jimmy Stewart. Especially the old James Bond films. But mostly she kept her unrequited love for Sean Connery a secret. She didn't want to encourage Dad to spend any more time with films and photographs.

"Especially photographs.

"'Jack, this hobby of yours is gonna put us in the poorhouse,' she'd scold. 'If you like that camera so much, why don't you follow around some movie stars with it? Like those poprot-zees?' Mom had a habit of mispronouncing words because she didn't care enough to learn them right.

"'What exactly is a "pop-rot-zee," Helen?'

"'Someone with a lot more money than us,' she'd snap.

"But Dad mostly ignored her. He thought that photographs should capture something special about the world. Something you can't put into words.

"'You know it when you see it,' he always told me. 'Like love. It's just there or it isn't.'" David pauses.

He doesn't look over at Allison. His eyes stay fixed on the road ahead. Even with everything that has happened, he has a calmness, an easygoing looseness that rubs off on Allison. It reminds her of the David she knew five years ago. Whenever she got scared or uneasy, she'd find David. He always knew what to do—like taking a walk to the creek to catch fogs or hiding out in the old tree house that Harold found. Those times were filled with talk about the past. About their lives before Jacob. About what they dreamed of doing when they grew up. David wanted to be a surgeon. Allison, a dancer.

"Your dad . . . ," Allison begins. "Your dad must have taken some great pictures."

"Well, he said he only took four pictures in his whole life that were worth a damn. And when he got to talking about those, he'd count them off: 'One, the way the sky looked on the day your grandma died; two, you asleep in your crib at seven months and twelve days; three, an empty milk bottle on the kitchen table in the late afternoon; and four, a homeless man asking for food in Atlanta.'

"'Why the last one?' I asked once.

"'There are no right words for the look on a man's face when the whole world has given up on him,' Dad said. 'No right words at all.'

"But the Leica M3 isn't my favorite just because of him," David says. "It's my favorite because it takes the most alive pictures you've ever seen. So alive that you wonder if you saw the real thing to begin with.

"At school there's an old-fashioned darkroom I can use for free. Well, it's more like a broom closet with aluminum foil over the window, but it's got all the equipment you need for developing black-and-white photos. The reddish light overhead. The chemicals that smell like opening a new textbook and sticking your nose right against the pages. Miss Garrett, the art teacher, lets me in after last period. She says that hardly anyone else uses it, and what a shame this and what a waste that. But I like having a quiet place to go to. Time practically stops in there. No sounds. No outside light. No one else around. It's just you and your pictures."

"That sounds nice," Allison says.

"Yeah." He nods. "I've taken thousands of pictures, but only one is worth a damn so far. Last spring I was in D.C. with my U.S. history class, and I saw this woman sitting on the steps of the Lincoln Memorial. She was by herself, dressed in a suit and smoking one of those clove cigarettes. There was something about her face that made me take a picture. About the way her left eyelid was heavier than her right.

"It's an honest moment. You can just see it." David pauses. "Dad would have liked that picture.

"I figure that's what he was looking for. Truth. You know, the capital *T* kind. The kind you only get glimpses of here and there because it doesn't come along very often. Just like taking a picture, I guess. It happens in a split second, and the rest of the time people are just pretending—pretending to be smarter or hotter or funnier or more important than they really are.

"Dad always said that it's damn important to be honest. That the world needs honest people right now more than ever. I believed him for a while. And when I saw how much he believed in Jacob, I did too."

Allison remembers feeling the same way about her own Dad. But faith is a tricky thing. It asks for more and more all the time. And everybody has to figure out just how much they can give.

Jacob taught her that. He taught all of them that.

As the road curves slightly ahead, Allison spots Jade's red Jeep parked at the side. The driver's door is open, and the brake lights glow red. There is nothing else around except trees.

"Look!" she yells.

But David already sees. He pulls up behind Jade's Jeep, and the car slows to a stop. When the engine shuts off, Allison can hear the forest buzzing with sound. A chorus of cicadas. Loud and fast. Coming and going. It's a frantic, urgent sound, she thinks.

Allison gets out of the car, and a thick humidity presses in around her. It's the kind that's so sticky you can hardly move.

The kind that makes you want the rain something bad.

She moves toward the Jeep and calls out, "Jade?"

Her voice echoes in the trees.

She takes another step and stops suddenly. David is right behind her.

"What?" he asks, looking at her face, then over to the Jeep.

Allison doesn't answer. A pool of blood stains the road. Red and thick. It drips from the car like a slow, leaky faucet.

David inches forward, as if someone might jump out and grab hold of him at any second. One step. Then another. He's about to reach the door when Jade's brake lights flicker.

Allison tenses.

The cicadas burst into a new scream, louder than before. She wants to cover her ears and scream herself. She wants to disappear, to be someone without any of this happening. Someone without a past that won't let go.

David leans into the open door now, slowly. He grabs the roof for balance, and Allison notices the blood pooling at his feet. He looks inside.

The color leaves his face.

Allison rushes forward to see for herself. Blood has sprayed all over the dashboard and front seat. Some has splattered on the windshield as well. It drips from the rearview mirror and the steering wheel. It covers the stick shift and the stereo.

But no one is in the car. Jade isn't here. Only her suitcase is in the backseat.

Allison is about to turn away when she sees something on the floor by the brake. It's hard to make out at first. Curled and jagged and bulky. She reaches down to pick it up. . . .

The silver rings.

The crooked fingers.

The blue nail polish . . .

It's Jade's hand. Cut off at the wrist.

Allison staggers, falling backward into a sitting position on the ground. Her hands and jeans are now sticky with Jade's blood.

She screams.

David helps her up, wrapping his arm around her shoulder and leading her to the car. Allison stumbles forward, heavy and awkward, and she can tell that David is practically carrying her. She collapses into the passenger seat, closing her eyes.

David hurries to the other side. She hears him fumbling with the keys, slamming the door behind him, and starting the ignition.

The engine roars.

The tires screech as they lurch onto the road.

Allison starts wiping her hands on her jeans, faster and faster. She wants to get the blood off, but it doesn't seem to help. It's as if her fingers are stained red. Permanently. There's blood on the leather seat beneath her too. She tries to wipe it away, but it seems to be everywhere.

David is speaking now. She can tell from the tone of his voice that he's trying to soothe her, but she can't make out the words.

Instead she imagines the photograph that he might have taken here. The red color of the Jeep bleeding onto the ground. And the strange beauty of Jade's tortured, twisted fingers.

11

DREAM JOURNALS

As soon as they get to David's room at the Whispering Winds, Allison rushes into the bathroom. She scrubs her hands in a kind of fever, rubbing the bar of soap hard against her palms. Rubbing until her hands practically disappear in the lather. Jade's reddish brown blood starts to run into the sink. Swirling around and around. Clinging to the rim. It's all over her clothes, too. Her shirt. Her jeans. Her shoes.

Allison yanks them off and throws them on the floor.

She is crying now.

The tears have been building since the news of Harold, since finding Emma's body. And now with Jade's Jeep. Hard, round drops slide down Allison's face. She can taste the saltiness of some on her tongue; others fall into the basin and mix with the blood and the soap.

She watches the water for a few moments and waits—until her eyes dry a bit. Until the blood disappears into the drain. Soon there's just a steady stream of water pouring from the faucet. Clear and cool.

As if nothing happened.

Allison splashes her face

In the mirror she sees herself standing there in her underwear, her hands dripping with water. They still feel dirty to her, and she rubs them hard with a towel. She looks tired and *much* older than seventeen. Her face reminds her of Ma. The way the lines around her eyes and mouth used to get real deep when she was lost in thought. Allison has her mother's face, she admits. The same brown hair and green eyes. The same narrow nose and small ears. But Allison never thought she'd look like the older version of Ma. That's what the face in the mirror makes her think of.

The older version.

It seems so unfair, though. To look like someone you've spent years trying to forget. She'd rather see hints of Daddy in her face. His sideways smile. His crooked front teeth. Anything but Ma. And what if looking like Ma means that Allison will act like her one day too? Will she also abandon the people who love her most? Will she shatter their hearts?

Not if she can help it.

Allison studies the lines on her face again, then looks at the meandering scar across her neck. Thin and narrow and slithery like a garden snake. *Ma never had one of these,* Allison thinks. Whatever scars Ma had from Mel seemed hidden. She never stuck around long enough for them to show.

All of a sudden Allison realizes that something is out of place. Something is missing.

Her scarf.

She glances at the floor and the countertop. It's not with the rest of her clothes. Maybe it fell off by the Jeep or in the passenger seat of her car, she thinks. She has to find it. She can't lose the scarf Bo gave her.

Bo.

Her time with him feels like it was part of another life.

They usually text-message two or three times a day, she and Bo, and he has probably left several messages on her useless cell phone by now. But what could she talk to him about, anyway?

The end of the world?

Her unfaithful heart?

Maybe she has more in common with Ma than she'd like to admit.

Allison turns off the faucet, and she can hear David talking to Sheriff Cooper on the phone. His words run together fast. David tried his cell in the car with no luck, so they raced here. It was the nearest place they could think of with a phone.

Besides, Allison was still hoping to see Ike sitting in front of David's door. Waiting for them with a Where-the-hell-have-you been? smirk on his face. Instead they pulled up to an empty hotel. No cars in the lot. No sounds, not even from the winds.

And no Ike.

Allison wipes her face again. Her eyes are puffy and red, but there's nothing she can do about that now. She grabs a thick towel from the back of the door and wraps it around her chest. It hangs a few inches above her knees.

She opens the door.

David's room is identical to Jade's and Emma's. The same comforter and cheap furniture. The same posters with purple and blue flowers. Something about the sameness makes Allison uneasy. So much has happened, so much has changed, she thinks, but you'd never know it from this room.

David is leaning over the end table. The phone cord is too short for him to stand up straight, and it looks like he's speaking into the lampshade. It's ridiculous and cute at the same time.

"It's just a couple of miles from here on Route Fifty-four," he says into the receiver. "I don't know . . . I don't know where he is either. . . ."

David switches the receiver to his other hand and reaches for his duffel bag on the puffy chair. He shuffles through a few things until he pulls out an inhaler.

"Room fifteen . . . Allison is with me."

Hssst.

He sucks in the medicine and holds it for a moment. His entire chest inflates. "Okay, we'll be here."

David hangs up and turns toward Allison. His eyes

widen at the sight of her wearing only a towel. "Um . . . Sheriff Cooper is on the way."

"I figured," Allison says, lingering by the bathroom. "Could you get my bag from the car? I need some new clothes."

"I figured," David says. He takes a step toward the door, then stops. "Who do you think survived the fire that night?"

"I don't know," Allison replies, shaking her head. "But if Linda's right, the whole town could be caught up in this somehow."

"With the killings?"

"Maybe they're just *letting* these things happen. . . ." Allison hesitates. "I don't know."

"Even the sheriff?" David's voice sounds hollow.

"Even the sheriff," she echoes.

David looks at her towel again. "I'll grab your stuff."

As he leaves the room with her keys, Allison glances outside. It's dark from the coming storm, and the gray clouds look like water balloons ready to burst. Suddenly the sky cracks with thunder. Loud and angry. The rumble shakes the walls of the Whispering Winds and fades into an echo.

Allison plops down on the edge of the bed. A few seconds later David comes back with her duffel bag in one hand and his inhaler in the other. He sits down next to her, putting the bag on the floor between them.

"Thanks," Allison says as she eyes his inhaler. "You still need that much? I haven't seen you use it yet."

"Hardly ever. I'm not sure why I keep it. A few years ago some doctor in Philadelphia told me that the prescription I had as a kid was a placebo. My pediatrician must have thought it was all in my head." He pauses. "Weird, huh?"

"What?"

"Thinking something is so real—life-or-death real—and finding out it's total bullshit."

Allison takes hold of David's hand. It's warm and moist.

"You mean Jacob?" she asks softly.

"I don't know. . . . Everything, I guess."

Another crack of thunder shakes the room, and David squeezes her hand. He looks into her eyes.

"I never told you what happened to me that day."

"When?"

"At the Confessional. I never . . . I just didn't want to think about it. But now . . ."

Allison puts her other hand on his.

"Now," he continues, "I can't get it out of my head."

At first David didn't mind the woods and the campsite because they were so quiet. It was like the exact opposite of his old house, which he considered the noise capital of North Carolina. That's because his mom was a yeller. Loud words and wild hand gestures—that's how she dealt with the world. It's not that she was particularly angry or upset twenty-four hours a day. Not at all. She was just loud.

That's the thing with yellers. They think the world can't hear them unless they're shouting at the top of their lungs. And after a while they don't even realize they're shouting anymore.

That was his mom.

So David figured that she wouldn't last five minutes in a quiet place like Jacob's camp. That he would be home before the first "Hallelujah" or whatever.

But the more Jacob talked, the quieter his mom got.

In fact, most adults seemed to clam up around Jacob, whether he was talking or not.

That eventually happened to the kids, too. During the final few months of the cult Jacob started having them write down their visions in silence. After that, Jacob took away their papers and never mentioned them again. This made David uneasy. What if Jacob finally learned something from their dreams after all? Something terrible.

David couldn't remember much about his dreams back then. It was like they were gone as soon as Jacob read them. But not the day Allison came back. . . . On that day, he could remember every detail.

The words just poured out of him, like he couldn't write them fast enough. And when Jacob came to the cabin to collect their journals, David held on to his tight. He watched the cult leader move from the back bunks to the front. Taking everyone's pages.

"Thank you, Emma," Jacob said.

"Thank you, Jade. . . ."

He was standing in front of Harold when David reached under Ike's mattress. David knew that Ike kept a couple matchbooks there from his trips to town, so he grabbed one and ran. He didn't know where he was going or what he was going to do exactly.

But he couldn't give his dreams to Jacob anymore.

By the time David got to the well, his journal was totally crumpled. It was so cold out that he was shaking all over. The dampness made it hard to light the matches too. He tried a bunch of them, but none would take.

Finally David got one.

The pages flared up, and he waited until the whole thing was burning good before he dropped it into the well. Jacob saw that part. David's dreams in flames, falling into the waterless well.

"Why?" Jacob yelled.

"Because . . . they're mine!" David blurted out. It was the only thing he could think to say.

With that, Jacob turned around and left.

The Doctor didn't come for him until after dinner. He was waiting outside the dining hall. He didn't speak. He didn't have to. David knew right away that it was his turn for the Confessional.

The Doctor always seemed to appreciate quiet things, David remembers. And they walked the entire path without a word. David felt grateful for the silence. It would've been a lot harder if the Doctor had said something. Sometimes talking just makes things worse. Most people don't understand that. But the Doctor did.

At the shed, he put his hand on David's shoulder, stopping him from going inside.

"No. Around back," he said. "Jacob is waiting for you there."

A thick blanket of leaves covered the ground. David could still make out the vivid colors in the twilight—reds, oranges, yellows, and browns. Ivy clung to the walls of the Confessional, and the whole thing was a lot longer than David had realized. It went right into the hill of black stone.

Then he saw Jacob standing there in his white suit—about fifteen or twenty feet in front of him. Not moving at all.

"Come," Jacob said, his voice cold and somehow magnetic.

David remembers taking one slow step, then another. And the whole time Jacob kept talking.

"Your visions, David, are not private things. They're not just your own." Jacob tilted his head back and looked up at the sky. "No. Your visions come from some place greater than this. From some being greater than us. And you have a responsibility to share them. . . ."

The leaves seemed to get deeper and thicker with every step.

"You had a real vision this morning, didn't you? Something important." Jacob lowered his head. "Something prophetic."

David took another step, and—

Swoosh.

The ground opened like a trapdoor.

Leaves and branches and dirt spilled on top of him as he tumbled into the opening. David tried to get up, but the back of his head hurt bad from the fall. That's when he noticed the smooth surface beneath him. Not dirt, but something else. Wood. Some kind of plank.

Right then a door closed above him, and everything got pitch black.

He was trapped in a small, tight space. Walls on all sides of him. He could hardly move.

That's when he realized that it wasn't a door that had closed. It was a lid.

He was in a coffin.

David's lungs started to tighten. He remembers trying to catch his breath, but he couldn't stop coughing from the dirt. There wasn't enough air.

He started pounding and kicking and screaming. He pushed his hands and knees against the lid. But it wouldn't budge. There was a heavy weight on top. It got harder to breathe, and his head was spinning.

For a second everything got still, and he tried to listen for Jacob. For any sound at all. *Jacob will let me out, David told himself. He wouldn't just leave me. He couldn't.*

David started to cry out for help, but that's when he heard the sounds. Not from outside. Not from above. But from inside the coffin.

Scurrying and clicking . . .

They were everywhere. All at once, it seemed. Not just sounds, but movement—things crawling up and down his body. On his chest and arms. On his neck. His face.

David swatted at them. He tried to roll over, to get away, but there wasn't enough room.

Then he heard a loud crash on top of the lid. He made himself get still. There was a heavy noise right above him. He tried to listen.

Thump.

It's Jacob, David thought. *It's over. He's going to save me.*

Thump.

Thump.

Then David figured out the sound. He finally knew what was happening.

Thump.

Dirt was falling onto the lid in heavy clumps. Jacob wasn't going to save him after all.

He was going to bury him alive.

David could feel hot tears all over his face. His whole body seemed to be covered with moving, biting things.

Pinching and burning his skin.

He pounded on the lid again. He knew it wouldn't do any good, but still he kept pounding.

After that David shut his eyes, like closing the shutter of a camera. He figured if he didn't see it, if he didn't take a picture of it in his mind, maybe it wouldn't be real. Maybe he would survive. . . .

David stops talking. His body is still, and he looks at the floor. Allison can see tears on his nose and upper lip. She wonders if he wants to reach for his inhaler. If the memory of being buried alive is enough to bring on an attack. It would be for her. But he doesn't move.

The inhaler stays on the bedspread.

"I don't know what happened after that," David adds. "I woke up in the infirmary. The Doctor told me I had been asleep for almost two days. Then he asked if I'd had any new dreams, but I honestly didn't remember any."

The thunder outside crashes again. This time rain follows, pounding heavy and fierce against the rooftop and the ground outside.

"Sorry," he says. "It's weird talking about it after all this time."

"That's okay. I'm glad you told me."

Allison gazes at David's face. The hard angles and faraway stare are handsome and sad at the same time. She understands the sad part. You don't have to live long to know that the deepest scars can't be seen. Sure, being marked on the outside sucks. But at least people know something happened. An accident. An illness. The cruelty of another. With a scar like Allison's, people don't assume everything is fine all the time.

But not for David. Like Allison's mother, he carries his scars on the inside. And it's tough for most folks to understand what they can't see.

"So," she says, "what did you write in your journal? The one you burned?"

"Oh . . ." David hesitates for a moment. "It was about the night you tried to steal my asthma medication from Jacob's box."

David turns to her, letting go of her hand. "I always thought you hated me for that. For what Jacob did to you . . . Even on the way back here I wondered if you still did?"

He says the last part as a question, and she can see the uncertainty in his eyes. Allison never considered blaming David for anything. They have all carried around so much guilt for so long, she thinks. For killing Jacob. For the death of their parents. Allison can't believe that David has been holding on to this, too.

Yes, she wanted to help him that night. That's why she went. But the box was filled with things that Jacob had no right to. Things that belonged to all of them. Things she wanted to take back.

"No," Allison replies, "I hated Jacob."

She reaches for his face, to wipe away some of the wetness from his tears, and David kisses her.

His lips are warm. His mouth and tongue taste better than chocolate chocolate chip ice cream. Cool and sweet.

A guilty pleasure.

Being this close. Breathing him in. Kissing him. It all sends chills down her body, and she wonders how she has lived her entire life without this feeling—when your whole body is so into someone that you can't think of anything else.

David touches her face now, and Allison presses her palms against his chest, mostly to keep from falling over with desire. One of his hands slides down to her shoulder, the other to her breast. He cups it gently.

She leans into him—

THUD. THUD. THUD.

The sound makes her jump.

"Police," a voice calls out from the other side of the door.

"Damn," Allison mutters, grabbing some clothes from her bag. "Turn around."

"What?" David asks.

"I gotta put something else on."

"Oh, yeah . . ." David looks at her, smiling, then turns his head. "I forgot."

"Sure you did."

Allison could just eat him up, she thinks as she sets a new world record for getting dressed when you don't want to get caught with a guy.

THUD. THUD. THUD.

"Coming," David calls out.

As she watches him walk to the door, she thinks she'd give just about anything in the world for a few more minutes of feeling his lips pressed against hers, for a few more minutes of forgetting about the fear inside her.

12

THE PORTRAIT OF
MRS. J. P. NORRINGTON

Allison hasn't seen David since they got to the Meridian Police Department. She can still taste him on her lips, though. She can feel his touch all over and picture the scar underneath his chin. She never noticed it before—the small, crescent-shaped scar. Maybe it's from those things that bit him in the coffin, Allison guesses. Maybe it's a nick from shaving or a fall from skateboarding. She wants it to be the kind of thing that happens to guys all the time. Something normal. Not a mark from Jacob's hand, just an ordinary scar. Something that an ordinary girl would notice about an ordinary boy she's falling in love with.

"David Holloway," she whispers. The syllables dance lightly on her tongue.

She is waiting in the same room, the same chair, where Sheriff Cooper took her statement about thirty minutes ago. It must have been a den when the last mayor lived here, Allison figures. Several oak bookcases are filled with novels and plays you wouldn't expect to find in a police station. Some stuff she's read in school, too—*The Crucible, The Old Man and the Sea, Catcher in the Rye, To Kill a Mockingbird*. There's a small oak table in the center with two matching chairs.

Across from her a portrait of an old woman hangs on the wall. She wears a plain gray dress and a silver necklace with a ruby pendant. Not the kind of outfit most folks would choose for a picture, Allison thinks. But she shouldn't talk. Back at the hotel she threw on a wrinkled floral skirt and a white tank top. The blue scarf almost matches the blues in her skirt. Almost. Her hair is a damp mess from the rain, and she could use some serious makeup.

Deputy Archibald enters the room. His forced smile reminds Allison of someone who has to go to the bathroom. When he sits down, he makes a slight grunting sound. Raindrops have left dark stains on his light brown shirt. He doesn't wear a hat like the sheriff, and his blond hair falls flat and square across his forehead.

He leans back just far enough to see her whole body, especially her legs. She doesn't like his hungry eyes. She has seen that look on guys before—mostly when she's around her best friend, Heather, but sometimes it's for her, too. It's the kind of looking that feels like touching—when you don't want to be touched.

"It must be real hard bein' back here," he begins, his words heavy and thick like the humidity. "After all this time. Of course, I only moved to Meridian a few years ago, so I wasn't around when y'all were up at that campsite. I remember seeing it on the news, though. About the cult. The fire. All those dead bodies."

Allison remembers the strength of the flames that night. It was hot enough to knock a person over, but that was nothing compared with losing her daddy. That pain still burns too deep to extinguish.

"That's gotta do somethin' to a person," Deputy Archibald continues, glancing again at her legs. "All that loss. All that talk about the end of the world. You think it's true?"

Allison tucks her legs under her chair. "What?"

"You think the world's going to end?"

"No." Her voice sounds more confident than she feels.

Deputy Archibald nods, and the constipated smile comes

back to his face. "That's kind of strange, don't you think?"

"What?"

"You not believin' . . . but here you are anyway. You and your friends." He pauses, as if he just asked a question.

"I didn't come here for the end of the world. Where's the sheriff?" Allison asks abruptly. It's the only thing she can think of to get out of this room—to get away from the deputy's probing eyes and sagging voice.

"Don't you worry. He'll be right along."

"Well, I want to talk to him. Not you."

"I saw the Jeep, Allison," he says. "All that blood. Jade's hand. We still haven't found the rest of her, though. Of course, she might be alive. There might be time to save her—"

"So what are you waiting for?" Allison snaps.

Deputy Archibald's smile dries up. "For you to start telling the truth."

"About what? I didn't do anything—"

"Why are you back here?"

"Harold's funeral . . . ," Allison starts, but she doesn't know what to say next. She's no closer to understanding what happened to Harold and Emma and Jade. She's no closer to knowing if Jacob was right after all. Her hands start to shake. "To say good-bye."

"I see. . . . Well, there certainly has been a lot of that lately. With all your friends getting killed, I mean. Just like old times."

His words hit her like a slap.

"Screw you!"

He leans forward, resting his elbows on the table. "It seems like you have quite the temper, don't ya?"

"Just a low threshold for stupidity."

The deputy chuckles. "In that case, why don't we cut to the chase? Seeing as you're so smart and all."

Allison doesn't speak.

"I think . . . ," he begins slowly. "I think you wanted to kill all those people five years ago when you started that fire. And I think you have something to do with what's going on now."

"No."

"We found your clothes in the bathroom, Allison. Soaked in blood."

"But—"

"How long do you think it's gonna take us to match that blood with the blood we found in the Jeep?"

"David and I were there. We told you that. *We* called *you!*"

"There'll be plenty of time for excuses later. Right now you need to tell me the truth. About where Jade is. About your other friend, Icarus."

"Ike," Allison mutters.

"Pardon?"

"His name is Ike, not Icarus," Allison says, practically spitting the words. "And I have no idea where they are."

She stands up, holding the edge of the table.

"Sit down," the deputy commands.

Allison can see his body tense, but she doesn't move. "Jacob killed my daddy five years ago. Jacob killed all those people that night," she says, her voice shaking. "Not me. Not any of us—"

"Sit down, I said," he barks, and the sharpness of his voice makes Allison drop back into her seat.

"Everyone around here is afraid of what's happening," he says. "Too afraid to see what's right in front of them, but not me. I know what you're trying to do—"

"What do you mean, 'afraid'? Afraid of what?"

All of a sudden the door swings open and Sheriff Cooper hurries inside. His pudgy face is flushed and sweaty, as if he has just been running. "Deputy, I need to talk with Miss Burke for a minute. Alone."

"I'm not finished with my questions—"

"Yes, you are."

The Sheriff stands there, breathing heavy and resting his hands on his hips. He watches Deputy Archibald with eyes as cold as the old woman's in the portrait.

"We'll finish this some other time," the deputy says to Allison as he gets up. "I promise."

"Joshua," Sheriff Cooper calls out, and the deputy leaves the room with sluggish, reluctant steps. He closes the door behind him.

Sheriff Cooper doesn't sit. He lingers halfway between the door and the table. "It's time for you and your friend to go," he says.

"What do you mean?"

"It's time for you to leave town. Understand?"

"Yeah."

"Good. Because if I see you again after tonight, I'm gonna let Deputy Archibald arrest you for murder."

Murder? The word makes Allison feel like she's riding in a car with someone who just slammed on the brakes. It was the word folks used to describe what she and the other kids did back then. Maybe it's true, Allison thinks. Maybe killing Jacob makes her a murderer. But she did it to save herself and her friends. To save her daddy.

Shouldn't reasons count for something?

"You think I had something to do with Jade?" she asks, fighting back her tears and anger. "Or Emma?"

"Deputy Archibald does. And when he sinks his teeth into something, he's as stubborn as a pit bull." Sheriff Cooper motions with his hand for her to get up. "Come on, now. I'll drop you off at the hotel so you can pack up."

Allison pushes back from the table and glances at the elderly woman in the portrait. Her dry, long face and black eyes seem more alive now—as if she has been watching all along.

"Sheriff?"

"Yes?"

"Who is that, anyway?" Allison asks.

The sheriff turns toward the painting. "That's Mrs. J. P. Norrington. At the turn of the nineteenth century she was mayor for a short while—until some folks around here started saying she was a witch."

"A witch?"

"Yup."

"So . . . what happened to her?"

"One night she was burned at the stake. Right in the middle of the town square." Sheriff Cooper looks back at Allison. "We've known a lot of sadness here."

Looking closer, Allison thinks that Mrs. J. P. Norrington has a smirk on her face. Kind of like the pictures she's seen of the *Mona Lisa*. Both of them seem to be women with secrets. Both of them seem to be women who like having secrets.

As Allison leans closer, the portrait bursts into flame. The canvas curls. The paint bubbles. And Mrs. J. P. Norrington's mouth opens in a silent scream. With her body burning, her face changes too. It becomes more youthful, more masculine—

Allison's body jolts. Her mouth is dry, and her tongue feels thick. She blinks several times to figure out what is real.

Suddenly the painting appears to be fine. Mrs. J. P. Norrington is elderly again. There is no fire.

Sheriff Cooper is watching Allison closely now. "Let's go," he says.

"Was she?" Allison asks.

"Was she what?"

"A witch?"

Sheriff Cooper pauses before opening the door for Allison.

"She was someone who didn't understand how fear changes people."

"So they were afraid of her?" Allison asks, not entirely sure what the sheriff is getting at.

"Most folks are afraid of what they don't understand. . . . Now, come on. I have to get you back to the hotel."

13

WINGS OF WAX

David starts packing as soon as they get back to the Whispering Winds. He shoves his clothes into the duffel bag with a swoosh and tosses it on the bed—the bed where they kissed and sat close and felt like normal teenagers for a while. Now it just looks empty, Allison thinks. Empty and like nothing happened at all.

She doesn't have to listen hard to hear David's breathing from across the room. It reminds her of a squeaky cat toy now. Wheezing and whistling. The kind that John Donne, the Packers' big white fur ball, plays with.

"I don't understand," he says as he checks the dresser drawers again. "Why did they let us go?"

"We didn't do anything—"

"We were the last people to see them alive!"

"Ike could be fine," Allison says flatly.

In truth, she *needs* Ike to be okay. She needs David's calmness, too. His soft voice and easy way with the world.

David glances at her before opening the desk drawer and taking out the phonebook. "If the sheriff wants us out of town so badly, why didn't he wait around for us to pack and leave?" David asks without looking up. "It just doesn't make sense," he adds with an *I'm sorry I snapped at you* voice. "That's all."

"Not unless he believes."

"Believes what?"

"Deputy Archibald said something really weird," Allison

says, watching David as he flips through the book in front of him. "He said that everyone here was afraid."

"Afraid of what?"

"I'm not sure, but what if Sheriff Cooper . . . what if the people around here believe that Jacob was right? Like Linda was saying at the library."

"That God is doing this?"

Allison nods. "That the end is coming, and there's no stopping it."

David tears a page from the phone book in a quick motion. "I just thought of what Jade would say about that theory," he says.

"With or without the bad words?"

David laughs, but it's over quick.

They both get quiet.

"I say we make one last stop in Meridian," David suggests as he hands her the page and points to a name near the bottom: Marcum P. Shale, 2818 Ezekiel Lane.

Something about the address seems familiar to her, but she's not sure why.

"He's listed?"

"Looks like it," David says as he grabs both of their bags and walks over to the door.

"Why didn't I think of that?"

"You were too busy putting the moves on me."

Allison feels her cheeks flush. "Yeah, right."

Outside it's dark, and the damp wind raises goose bumps on Allison's arms and legs. She can't remember a September night ever being this cold. Usually you can feel summer all month long, holding on for dear life. But not tonight. Tonight the air is winter cold, and the gray clouds move across the sky like crowds of people pushing one another forward.

Allison gets to her car quickly.

The wind picks up all of a sudden, and it carries a strange noise from the wall of trees behind her. Not the whistling winds or an ominous melody. Something else. A muffled cry. A moan.

"Do you hear that?" Allison asks.

"Yeah."

The sound starts again. Louder this time. It reminds Allison of the nights she used to cry into her pillow so no one else could hear.

"Ike?" she calls out.

A branch cracks loudly—*snap*.

There is movement in the trees. Someone is running away. Fast.

"Ike!" Allison screams.

Without thinking, she runs into the forest.

It's much darker here. Wet branches and leaves slap her body. Scratching, biting, and clawing at her skin as she chases after the movement ahead.

"Slow down," David yells somewhere behind her.

But Allison can't stop herself. If Ike's out here and he's okay, then maybe she and David will be okay too. They have to find him. To help him.

She stumbles over a fallen trunk but doesn't lose her balance completely. The forest seems to be getting thicker and more aggressive, she thinks. Like it doesn't want her here.

Urrrrr.

The muffled yell is close now.

Allison pushes into a large, circular clearing. A tall, T-shaped post stands in the center with what looks like a scarecrow tied along the top. Its arms out. Frayed clothing hangs from its body.

The dark keeps everything in shadows.

Urrrrr.

The sound is coming from the scarecrow, Allison realizes.

Its head is moving side to side. She rushes forward and sees the disheveled, spiked hair. The round face. The wide eyes.

Ike.

"Ike," she says, happy enough to cry. "Don't worry. We'll get you down—"

Bright light and a wave of heat suddenly knock her to the ground. She can see Ike's sky blue eyes and freckled skin clearly now. His hair reminds her of orange flames. It illuminates his whole face.

But the sound . . . it isn't muffled anymore. It's piercing. A scream—a terrible, painful scream.

Ike's face shifts in the light. His skin is changing. Melting like Mrs. J. P. Norrington's. The white light turns red and orange. Fire scrambles up the pole. It's as bright as high noon in the desert. And hot—against her face, her legs. All over.

For a second Allison wonders if this is another trick, another seizure or vision, but no. It's different. The screams. The vicious heat . . .

It's real.

Ike is burning to death. Right in front of her.

"Allison!" David is pulling her back now, away from the fire. Toward the line of trees.

No, no, no, no . . .

Allison swings her arms to break free. David is saying something, but she can't hear anything over Ike's screams and the roar of the fire.

She starts to run. Back into the forest again. Faster than before. Frantic. Sweat gathers on her face and chest. Her skin is still warm from the memory of the flames.

She stumbles and falls. Hard. Something jagged cuts into the skin beneath her elbow. A stone.

She gets back on her feet, running again.

At the parking lot she hurries past the Dumpster and her

car. She remembers a fire extinguisher on the outside wall two doors down from David's room. *There*. There it is.

The rusty box opens easily. She grabs the heavy red canister and sprints back into the woods.

The light of the fire is spilling through the trees now, making the branches and leaves glow around her. Her heart is pounding. Her breath short and hard.

She stumbles back into the clearing again and struggles with the extinguisher in her hands—snapping the safety and removing the hose. She aims at the flames. . . .

Nothing.

She pulls the handle again.

Nothing.

She starts shaking the can.

"Come on!"

David is by her side. He takes the canister from her and points it toward Ike as well. No spray comes from the hose.

"It's broken," David says. "It's . . . it's too late. He's gone."

Allison falls to her knees. David's right, she realizes. There are no more screams. Only a shadowy outline of Ike hangs in the middle of the flames. It's not him anymore.

Allison starts clawing at the ground. The soil feels cool and forgiving against her skin. She wants to scream and cry, but can't. Everything is bright as day. The circle of trees huddle around like spectators. David is on his knees next to her.

They can't do anything now but watch. . . .

Allison gets up slowly and leads the way back to the hotel without a word. The smell of fire is thick in the air, and she can even see flakes of ash on the windshield of her car. She stands at the door, hands shaking as she reaches for the keys in her pocket.

"You're bleeding," David says.

Allison looks at the long stream of blood on her forearm. "I don't feel a thing."

"Come on." David touches her other arm gently, leading her back to room 15. "Let's take care of that."

Inside, Allison lingers by the door while David grabs a washcloth from the bathroom. He dabs it against the wound at first, then presses down strong.

"It's not that bad," he says, his voice shaky.

Allison looks at the keys in her hand and notices the crumpled page from the phone book there. Balled up. She opens it, staring at the name and address at the bottom. Something about it . . .

"What the hell happened back there?" David asks, still holding the cloth to her arm. "It's like he just burst into flames."

"Yeah," Allison says faintly, but she is far away now. Numb. She's not still picturing Ike in the clearing like David is. She's saying Marcum Shale's address over and over in her head. That number nags at her. There is something about it.

"We have to get out of here," David continues. "The cops are just going to blame us."

"Yes, we should go," Allison says.

David nods, obviously relieved. "Want me to drive first? I figure we can make it to Virginia in a couple hours, then—"

"No. We have to go here."

Allison hands David the paper. He stares at it for a few seconds.

"Are you out of your mind?"

"Maybe, but we have to—"

"Seriously. Are you fucking crazy? We have to get out of this town while we still can."

"While we still can?"

"Yeah!" David yells. "Before we end up dead."

"How far do you think we're going to get, huh?" Allison snaps back. "Five miles? Ten? It's not going to stop, David. We need answers, and this is the only place we're going to find them."

David turns away from her and exhales loudly.

"What makes you think this guy knows a damn thing?" he asks, forcing his voice to be calm.

Allison steps over to the nightstand and opens the drawer.

"What are you doing?"

"Read the address to me," she says.

"What?"

"Read Shale's address!"

"Twenty-eight eighteen Ezekiel Lane," David answers flatly.

Allison turns to him with the hotel Bible in her hands. "Ezekiel. Chapter twenty-eight, verse eighteen: 'Thou hast defiled thy sanctuaries by the multitude of thine iniquities, by the iniquity of thy traffic; therefore will I bring forth a fire from the midst of thee, it shall devour thee, and I will bring thee to ashes upon the earth in the sight of all them that behold thee.'"

Allison closes the Bible.

"He's gotta know something," she says.

14

THE UNSPOKEN

The car ride is postfight quiet—the kind of quiet that feels almost as bad as fighting. Uneasy. Electric. It's not like they're really mad at each other, Allison admits. They're just hurting from what they've seen, from what's been happening to them. But that doesn't change anything now.

Allison presses the cloth against her arm. It's still bleeding a little—that's why David insisted on driving.

"You know where you're going?" she asks with the voice she usually reserves for Brutus Packer Jr. on bad days or for creepy Bill Stevens, who sits behind her in chemistry class and blows on the back of her neck.

"I'll just look for the fire and brimstone." David's voice is colder than the air.

She deserves it.

The front windshield starts to steam up from their angry breathing. Well, that and because the defroster doesn't work. It has always been broken, and Allison has never gotten around to fixing it.

David wipes his forearm on the windshield before turning off the highway and heading back into the heart of Meridian. The town circle is empty and without light. She forgot what it's like to be in a place without streetlights. A place where everything is so dark at night.

The Confederate soldier eyes them as they swing around the circle and turn onto Maple Drive. Allison wonders if he was watching when the town chanted "Witch" and burned Mrs. J. P. Norrington at the stake. Would he have saved her if he could? Would he have looked for a fire extinguisher? Or just put a bullet in her head so she wouldn't have to suffer like Ike did?

Tears start to sting Allison's eyes, but she holds them back.

They pass several streets of quiet, dark houses. It's late for Meridian, Allison realizes as she glances at her watch. Almost ten o'clock. She can't believe it's the same day. Each minute has lasted a thousand years, and it's still not over. She turns to David, wanting to say something about the way time can be slow and stubborn. But he is staring at the road.

She closes her eyes.

Bedtime always came too early. At least that's how Allison remembers it. Both Melanie and her in pj's. Brushing teeth. Trying to hog the bathroom sink. Sometimes shoving each other when Daddy wasn't looking.

"Enough silliness, girls," he'd say, and they were off to bed.

Melanie in her room with the window overlooking the front yard. Allison in her room down the hall.

Daddy read stories to both of them before bed. Always in Mel's room—because she was the youngest, he'd say. His voice swayed when he read. Like the swing in their front yard. Back and forth and easy enough to carry you along.

Then they'd fold their hands for prayers.

"Keep our family safe from harm," he'd say, so soft that Allison always imagined God having to listen really hard to hear. Maybe that was the point. It's better to have someone listening close than only half listening. Or not at all.

"Bless Allison and Melanie, Ma and Daddy. Amen."

"Amen," the girls would echo.

Half the time Mel waited until she heard Daddy go to bed, then she'd sneak down the hall to Allison's room. The door would open real slow before Mel hurried over and hopped into her older sister's bed.

Mel had lots of bad dreams. Mostly about sharks. About how they never stop moving, not even to sleep. About how they're always feeding off things. Sometimes she was underwater with them, swimming and breathing just fine, but she was always afraid in those dreams—afraid one would get her.

When Mel talked about the sharks, Allison would stroke her sister's long brown hair until they both fell asleep.

Or until she wanted Mel to leave.

"It's time to go," she'd tell Melanie.

"I wanna stay."

"You have your own room. Go on, now."

Mel would climb out of bed, pouting and dragging her feet. "Dork," she'd mutter.

"Loser."

"Booger head."

"Vagina."

That was Mel's least favorite word, so Allison usually saved it for last. Mel always left after that.

Sure, there were times Mel didn't come down the hall to talk about her dreams or anything else—if they'd had a fight that day or if Daddy was real serious about bedtime. But after Allison's first seizure and her vision of Mel dying, Allison wanted her sister close.

She wanted to keep an eye on her.

It was getting late the night it happened. Daddy tucked them in, and almost an hour went by without any sign of Mel. Allison kept looking at the clock. The numbers glowing red and moving soundlessly from one minute to the next: 9:54 . . . 9:55 . . . 9:56 . . . 9:57 . . .

Allison just couldn't stand it anymore. She got out of bed and crept down the hall. It was so dark and quiet and cold. The wood floors felt icy against her feet. No wonder Mel didn't want to go back to bed alone.

The door to Mel's room was slightly open. The moonlight spilled in through the window, giving everything big shadows and an eerie white glow. Allison was about to call out to her sister when she saw something move.

It hovered over Mel's bed. Bigger than Daddy. Bulky and mean looking. It exhaled in snorts like an animal.

Allison's eyes adjusted, and she could see the outline of a man. He was wearing a coat that gave his body a strange shape. One hand pressing hard against Mel's mouth. The other came to a sharp point.

The pointed hand moved fast across Mel's neck, then the man stood up straight. He was almost tall enough to hit the ceiling with the top of his head. Allison could tell that he was looking at her now. She just stood in the open door, clutching her yellow blanket. She couldn't speak. She couldn't move, either. It was like her feet had finally frozen to the floor.

That's when he smiled.

It was the ugliest smile she had ever seen. The kind that would make you never want to smile again in your whole life. It stayed on his face as he stepped over to her. His pointed hand hanging at his side.

Something was dripping from it.

He leaned down, bringing his face close to hers. His eyes were black, and she could feel the hotness of his breath on her face.

"Next time," he whispered, the words coming out slow.

All of a sudden Allison could feel a warmth between her legs. Urine running down her legs and pooling on the floor. She looked down.

The man dropped something at her feet. Something wiry and sharp.

A second later he was gone.

Allison isn't sure how long it took her to move or why she can't remember anything more about his face than those black eyes. But when she picked up the untwisted coat hanger and felt the stickiness on her fingers, she could move again.

She ran to her sister.

Black blood covered her neck like a scarf. Her eyes were whiter than the moonlight. Allison screamed.

She screamed until Ma and Daddy burst into the room. But by then it was too late. Mel was gone.

A shark had gotten her after all.

Allison jolts up in her seat. At first she isn't sure if she just had a nightmare or a seizure. A sticky taste fills her mouth, but she doesn't feel dizzy or nauseous. No. It was a nightmare. A familiar one.

Later on the police explained that Mel had been strangled to death—that the coat hanger was used "after the fact." But knowing that has never made Allison feel any better. She still should've gotten to Mel sooner. She should've called out for help faster—

"You okay?" David asks.

Allison looks out the passenger window. There are fewer houses now and more trees along the roadside. She and David are getting toward the far end of town, she realizes. They're almost there.

"Yeah," she says. "Just thinking."

"About?"

"My sister." Allison continues to watch the road. "I've never been able to talk about what happened the night she died. Not really. It's like I can't, you know?"

David doesn't say anything. There is only the sound of the engine grumbling and the tires humming against the road. Every once in a while the glove box rattles like it always does.

"I think . . . ," David begins. "I think there's at least one thing in everyone's life that's too painful, too hard for words. For the right words, anyway. One thing that should stay . . ."

"Unspoken?"

"Yeah, unspoken."

Allison turns to David. "That's my unspoken, then. What happened that night."

David nods, then his expression changes. The car slows, and he pulls to the side of the road. Allison looks ahead. The headlights reflect off an old, weathered mailbox with the number 2818.

"I can't believe it," David says as he turns off the engine. "I was starting to think we wouldn't find it. That it wouldn't be a real address."

"Yeah."

They sit quietly for a few moments before David asks, "Now what?"

"I don't know," Allison replies. "I'm scared."

"Me too."

David reaches over and takes her face in his hands. Allison can tell that he is trying to say something—something to comfort them. Or something about her sister. Or maybe something about love.

But love can be an unspoken thing too, Allison thinks. Secret love. Forbidden love. Unrequited love. At least with love, there are other ways to communicate.

Allison leans in and kisses him.

His lips are surprised at first. Then warm and soft and eager.

The back of her head tingles.

When they finally pull away, David is smiling. They both are.

"You ready?" he asks.

"For what?"

"I have an idea," he replies, reaching for the handle to open the door.

But as Allison gets out of the car, she can't help but wonder if that was the last kiss she'll ever have. If that was an end-of-the-world kiss.

15

EZEKIEL LANE

Allison watches as David opens the trunk and grabs the tire iron.

"What's that for?" she asks.

"Insurance." David closes the trunk and looks at her. "Let's go up there and see what we can see. No rushing into anything, okay?"

Allison nods as they start walking up the dirt driveway. The broken stones and patches of mud make it hard not to trip. On both sides of the path trees and tall grasses buzz with sound— crickets, cicadas, and other moving things. It seems like too much noise for the dark, Allison thinks.

It takes a while before they see the front yard and the shadowy outline of a walnut tree. Its enormous branches spill outward from the trunk in all directions. Its leaves shake from the steady wind.

Somehow the tree seems blacker than the night sky.

Underneath there is a parked car. As Allison gets closer, she recognizes it from the funeral home and the hotel. It's rust colored. Marcum Shale must be the man with the flute, she figures. Her stomach knots fast with the memory of him walking toward her in the parking lot. The black coat wrapped around his body. His purple lips.

"Maybe this is a mistake," Allison mutters.

"You think?" David asks sarcastically, still moving forward.

"Seriously," she says.

David turns around. "It's like you said. This guy knows

something. And if he's responsible for what happened to the others . . ." His grip tightens on the tire iron. "We're just taking a look."

With that, David continues past the car and up to the front of the house. There isn't a single light coming from inside. The porch, which wraps around the first floor, is covered with scattered furniture—some beat-up chairs, a swing that looks ready to collapse at any second, boxes stacked here and there, a folded card table. It's not a porch for resting, Allison thinks. It's a place for discards. For junk.

"Let's check around back," David whispers.

All of the windows alongside the house seem boarded up—or at least covered by something on the inside. One has a shattered pane with only a few triangles of glass left. The siding is weathered and chipped. A tired roof sags over each side, and the storm gutters remind Allison of an open tin can. Rough and uneven.

As they move toward the rear of the house, she can see things more clearly. The shape of David's body. The plants and weeds at her feet. It's getting brighter, she realizes. A flickering light glows in the backyard.

All of a sudden David stops moving. He sees the light too. Allison hesitates.

"What is it?" she asks in a whisper, but he doesn't respond. She creeps forward to see for herself.

Inside the yard there is a circle of torches. Each one burns at the tip of a long staff. Six total. Gusts of cold wind push the flames sideways. Almost hard enough to snuff them out, but not quite. In the center there is a large pile of dirt.

"We have to get out of here," Allison says, grabbing David's arm. He was right back at the hotel, she thinks. They shouldn't be here. It's a mistake, a trap.

But David pulls away from her. He moves toward the dirt

with steady, plodding steps, as if he's in a trance.

"*David*," she pleads, but he doesn't stop.

The flickering light animates all the shadows around them. The trees. The closed-up house. Everything in the darkness seems alive and watchful now.

David gets to the center and stands perfectly still, staring at something beneath him. She finally understands what. There isn't just a pile of dirt in the circle, but a deep hole in the ground.

A burial plot.

Allison rushes forward. She has to get him out of here. She reaches the edge of the pit and glances inside. There is enough light to see movement below—fast and shimmering. For a split second she wonders if it's a stream of muddy water.

Then she makes out the rats. Rats fighting one another and clawing at the walls. Rats trying savagely to get out.

This time Allison clasps David's wrist and pulls.

"Come on!"

David turns toward her as something hits both of them. More jarring than electricity. Allison falls to the ground, twisting her left ankle. At the same moment David tumbles into the pit.

He's gone.

Now the man in black is standing there. The man from the parking lot. He holds a shovel in his hand. The shovel he used to hit David on the back of the head.

"I've been expecting you," he says.

16

THE END OF THE WORLD

The man tosses aside the shovel and bows his head, as if in prayer. His body is perfectly still. From here Allison can see his purple lips. The gray skin that seems so familiar. Hard and unforgiving.

The cold wind stings her face as she turns sideways and gets to her feet. Her ankle burns from the awkward fall, and her heart races with worry for David. She can't let this happen to him.

Not again.

She starts running toward the house and up the steps of the back porch, her ankle screaming in protest. Glancing over her shoulder, she can see the man behind her, still standing by the grave, but she doesn't slow down. She just pulls open the door and slams it shut behind her, turning the dead bolt.

I have to do something, she thinks as she looks around.

Inside the house isn't dark after all. The boarded-up windows make it seem that way from the outside, but several candles give off a low light. A few on the kitchen counter. Several in the dining room beyond that. Small, weak flames, but just enough to see.

The cabinets and counters look as worn as the exterior. Allison checks the drawers for a knife, for anything she can use to protect herself.

Nothing.

Each drawer is empty—as if they've never been opened before. The cabinets, too.

She doesn't see a phone.

The kitchen door rattles, followed by the dead bolt snapping open with a hollow clap.

He's using a key, Allison realizes as she limps quickly into the dining room.

A round table takes up most of the space here. It's almost completely covered with papers and yellow notepads. Three candles sit on a plate in the center—dark red and mostly hollowed out. The walls are lined with boxes and stacks of newspapers, just like the office at the library.

The living room is similar. Papers and books and boxes against most walls. Thick drapes cover the windows, which would otherwise look onto the massive walnut tree in the front yard. More than a dozen candles of different sizes glow on the mantel. A painting hangs on the wall above them. A painting of emptiness, Allison thinks. A barren landscape. Black and charred. Thin strands of smoke rising from the ground. Completely lifeless.

Allison can hear heavy footsteps in the kitchen now. The man is coming for her. Fast.

She darts into the hallway and heads for the door at the other end. The framed photographs covering the walls rattle as she rushes by. She can't make out the pictures in the dark, though. She holds out her hands, so as not to crash headfirst into anything. Then she reaches the door. The handle seems stuck at first. She twists it back and forth a few times before realizing that it's locked.

"Damn it!" she blurts out.

To her right the hall continues. To her left a staircase leads upstairs.

"Allison," the man calls out from the living room. He stands at the end of the hall, looking at her. His body thicker than the walls. His voice cold enough to freeze water. "You're the last one."

She takes the stairs two at a time, despite the pain in her ankle, despite the fact that she wants to run outside to David. He'll be okay, she tells herself. She can't be the last one.

"It's time," the man says, his voice already sounding too close.

At the top of the staircase Allison sees light coming from a room halfway down the corridor. There is another door at the far end, but it is closed. She hurries toward the light, slipping inside the nearby room and pulling the door shut behind her. Quietly. Her heart pounds. Her breathing is short and panicked.

This place is different from the rest of the house. It's clean and orderly. Nicely bound books fill several bookcases. The desk in the center is mostly cleared off. Two candles burn there, next to a jar filled with cloudy water and something else.

Allison picks it up.

The jar is heavy, and the glass is moist with condensation. She holds it over one of the candles to see more clearly.

Inside there is a hand soaking in formaldehyde. The fingers wiggle slightly from the movement.

Fingers with blue nail polish.

She screams, dropping the jar onto the desk. The glass shatters. Fluid spills onto the floor, and Jade's hand slides across the desktop.

The door swings open behind her.

"It's been a long time, Allison," the man says calmly as he pulls back his hood.

For the first time Allison can see his entire face clearly. The long, drooping face. The black eyes and gray skin. The half smile that makes you think you're safe when nothing could be further from the truth.

"Doctor?"

She moves to the other side of the desk, wanting to put something between herself and this ghost. Jacob's assistant.

The Doctor. The man who patched up wounds so Jacob could open them again.

"That is what you used to call me," he says, flat and cold.

"You survived the fire that night. *You.*" She thinks of the way his face looked when he bandaged her neck, when he said kind things on the way to the Confessional. None of that softness is there now.

She is seeing the *real* Doctor.

"You've been doing this all along," she says.

"No." He takes a step forward. "But I've been watching you for five years. All of you. Keeping track. Making preparations for the end."

"The end?"

"The prophecy is nearly fulfilled. You know this, Allison." The man nods slightly. "Praise be."

"Prophecy? That's what you call killing us one by one?"

"God is bringing about the end, not me. I'm merely . . . facilitating his plans."

"You really think God is going to end the world because some wacko said so five years ago? Jacob wasn't a prophet. He was . . . a liar. A liar and a killer. *Like you!*"

The Doctor starts to laugh, and his entire body shakes. It is an unsettling sound.

"Of course Jacob wasn't a prophet. Jacob was nothing. Less than nothing. When I found him, he was drunk and broke and eating out of garbage cans."

"What are you talking about!" she yells, her legs shaking as much as her voice.

"I knew there was something special about him, though. The way he could talk circles around most folks. A silver tongue, he had. A quick mind, too. He had been a teacher once—before he was fired for abusing some of his students. Jacob always had a bit of a temper," the Doctor says with a smile. "But I was able to help, you see. I cleaned him up. I taught him about faith and the Bible. I taught him about the end time and the need to prepare for the new world. And after he got his son back from his ex-wife, we moved to Meridian. Well, he came here first."

"Jacob wasn't a prophet?"

"No."

"What . . . what about his visions?"

"The only vision Jacob ever had was from a bottle of scotch." The Doctor chuckles. "At a certain point he had you write out your dreams so I could read them," the Doctor continues, his voice scratchy and intense and faint at the same time—like someone with laryngitis. "Jacob was only interested in learning about your nightmares. About your fears."

The Doctor pauses.

"Think of him as a mouthpiece. A spokesman for the truth. I needed someone with his charisma, someone with his gift for words. To get people to listen."

Allison's head is spinning. How can she believe any of this? That Jacob was the biggest lie of all? That she and Daddy and everyone else who was part of the Divine Path had just been fools?

She feels nauseated.

"It was all a *lie*?"

"Oh, no. My visions of the end—what I've seen, what I came to understand from your dreams. It's all true, Allison. I simply chose Jacob to be the voice. Like God giving the Commandments to Moses."

"I don't believe you. . . ."

"Real power is never where you think it is. It's never what it seems to be."

"Lies," Allison mutters. "Jacob. God. All the things we were told to believe. *You*—"

The Doctor lunges forward so quick that Allison doesn't have time to react. He clamps his hand around her neck and shoves her against the wall. The bookcases rattle. Allison tries to pry open his grip, but he just squeezes tighter. With his other hand he tears down the drapes covering the only window in the room.

"See for yourself," he hisses, pressing her face against the glass pane.

She struggles to breathe.

"Look!" he bellows.

In the yard below Allison can see the circle of torches and the rectangular plot in the center. Something is happening. The dirt. It's filling the hole—pouring in as if someone were shoveling it. But no one is there.

The dirt is moving . . . *on its own*. Thick, steady clumps lifting from the pile. Burying David with each passing moment.

"No," Allison says, shaking her head. "I don't believe it. I don't believe you!"

He throws her across the desk. Shards of glass from the jar bite into her back and legs. Then she hits the floor.

"Believe? It doesn't matter what you believe." The Doctor spits out the words. "You and your friends are the final sign. The sacrificial lambs. And with your death, Allison, a great fire will consume the earth—"

"*No!*"

"Nothing can stop it. Even if I let you walk out of here right now, there are still ninety-three days until the year's end. Ninety-three days for your greatest fear to find you. To consume you. It is his will."

Ninety-three days.

The words buzz in her ears. She hadn't thought of it like that. After the e-mail about Harold, Allison figured she'd either survive coming back to Meridian or she wouldn't. She never imagined another ninety-three days of being afraid. She shakes her head again.

"Still a doubting Thomas," the Doctor says, taking a step toward her. "How do you explain what happened to your friends, then? And what about your mother? Leaving you and your daddy for a nice little place in Florida, right outside of Tallahassee."

"What?"

"Well, I had to keep an eye on her, too. You never know when guilt will get the better of a person, when a mother might come looking for her daughter."

"You know where Ma is? You saw her?" Allison gets into a sitting position. Her right thigh is bleeding bad. A large fragment of glass is next to her. She takes it in her hand.

"Yes. And the man she had an affair with."

Tears start flooding Allison's eyes, making the room blurry. "That's not true."

"She got pregnant," the Doctor continues. "Of course, she got rid of the baby."

"Liar!"

"The problem was she didn't tell the father. That's why he came to your house that night—when he found out. That's why he killed Melanie. An eye for an eye, Allison."

"Stop. . . ." Allison gets to her feet, backing away from him. The anger and confusion pulsing through her body. Her lips quiver. Her arms and legs tense.

"I have something for you." The Doctor opens the desk drawer, and his hand lingers for a moment. Then he takes out a long wire, sharpened at one end.

An untwisted coat hanger.

"You recognize this, don't you?"

Allison backs into the hallway through the doorway,

shaking her head. She can feel the glass cutting into her hand, but she doesn't care.

"I had a chat with Mr. Hascom," he presses, walking toward her with the coat hanger in his right hand. "That was his name. Roger Hascom. He followed your ma to Florida, but she wouldn't have anything to do with him. Broken, he was. That can make a man dangerous. Having no hope left."

The Doctor stops in the doorway.

"I couldn't take the chance that Roger would come looking for you," the Doctor continues without moving. "That he would kill you like he killed your sister. To take away what your mother took from him. So I paid him a visit."

"You . . . killed him?"

"He is at rest now. It was the only way to protect you, Allison. To protect the prophecy."

"What about—"

"Your mother? She's still an empty shell. Too dazed by pain to be much good to anyone. All that guilt about the affair. About her own daughter's murder. It can eat a person from the inside out."

Allison's head is spinning. She runs toward the staircase, not sure what to do. The Doctor is following close behind her. She just reaches the first step when he shoves her against the wall. Her head smashing into the plaster. She can feel it give way.

She turns, and the sharpened coat hanger cuts across her neck. It digs into the skin, rough and uneven. The strength leaves her legs.

She collapses to the floor. Head spinning. Her vision blurry.

His black boots are caked with mud, and so is the bottom of his overcoat. He holds the coat hanger by his side now. She can see her own blood on it. Dripping in slow, heavy drops to the floor. Allison presses one hand against her neck. It is warm with blood. The other burns from the glass shard that she still squeezes there.

The Doctor squats and presses the coat hanger against her cheek.

"I wonder what your sister was thinking that night," he whispers. "Was she too terrified to scream? Or was she waiting for you? For her big sister to save her?"

Allison can feel something surging inside her—rage and hatred. For this man. For all the guilt and pain. For Mel and Ma and Daddy. Suddenly Allison thrusts the broken glass into his neck. She drives it deep into the skin and keeps pushing, even as he falls backward onto the floor.

The Doctor drops the coat hanger and reaches for the glass in his neck. Air comes out of his nose and mouth like a high-pitched whistle. His eyes wide with surprise. His teeth clenched as he tries pulling out the shard.

Allison starts crawling toward the stairs, but the Doctor grabs her ankle. With one yank he pulls her back. Allison's face slams against the floor, and her skirt slides up around her waist.

She picks up the coat hanger.

The Doctor pulls her again. This time his clammy hands lock on to the backs of her thighs. His fingers digging deep into her flesh. He rolls her over.

He has removed the glass from his neck, and blood pours fast from the wound. His eyes wide as he looks up and down her body. At her bare legs and underwear. At her torn shirt. At the blood on her neck.

The Doctor is swallowing her up with his eyes, Allison realizes. He doesn't look at her the way a hungry man looks at food. He looks at her with greed. Like someone who is ready to take something that doesn't belong to him. For a split second she imagines him watching Emma and Jade and Harold and Ike with those insatiable, thieving eyes.

He grabs both of her legs again and pulls her closer to his body.

Allison shoves the coat hanger into his left eye.

"Ahhh!"

Allison reaches the handrail and starts pulling herself down the stairs. To get away from the horrible screams. To get away from his body writhing on the floor. She slips and falls down two or three steps, landing on her knees.

When she gets to the bottom of the staircase, the Doctor has gotten silent.

She looks up.

His body is still.

Allison limps through the dark hall—past the living room and into the kitchen.

Outside the strong wind makes the torch flames cower and blink. It still carries some dirt into the hole, but not the same way. It no longer looks like an invisible force shoveling clumps into the open grave.

Allison rushes over to the pit. The lid of the coffin is closed, but some of the yellowish pine is visible through uneven layers of dirt. She can still get to him, she thinks. There's still time.

Allison grabs the shovel on the ground and lowers herself onto the coffin. She gets down on her knees and starts wiping away the dirt. There are a few inches of space surrounding the coffin, and Allison tries to push most of the dirt into those gaps.

"David!" she yells. "Can you hear me?"

She pounds her fists on the lid several times.

"David!"

She pounds again.

Nothing.

She stands up, grips the handle of the shovel with both hands, and starts to smash the metallic scoop into the wood. Up and down. With all the strength in her arms and shoulders. Smashing and pounding. Moving in a frenzy.

Crack—a board gives way.

Crack. Crack.

"David!" she yells as another board snaps beneath her.

There is a hole in the wood now, and she strikes it again. Out of the opening a rat scurries toward her.

Allison screams, swatting at it with the shovel.

Several more follow.

"David," she calls out again as the rats race toward the walls of the pit and try to climb out.

She wedges the shovel into the hole and moves the handle up and down. A piece of the lid snaps off—wide enough for a basketball to fit through.

Rats and beetles spill out from inside the shattered wood. They're everywhere now. All around her feet. Scrambling. Then she hears a thumping beneath her.

"David?"

A hand suddenly reaches through the opening, and he starts pushing against the lid. *He's alive,* she thinks.

"Hold on," she yells as she starts to claw at the loose dirt and grass, pulling herself up and over the edge.

David pushes open the lid in an instant, gasping for air as if he has been held underwater. He swats at the rats on his body.

"David," she says, holding out her hand.

But he pulls himself onto the grass next to her.

His face is scratched and bleeding from bite marks. He runs his fingers over his face and ears and neck. His movements are frantic. His eyes wide with fear.

"I can still feel them all over!"

"It's okay," Allison says.

But his body is shaking, and he still swats at his skin.

"It's okay," she says again, grabbing his shoulders. "It's over."

He looks at her, blinking fast.

"You're safe now."

"No . . ."

His body still twitches. He pushes back from her and stands up, brushing at his clothes. His eyes dart back and forth.

"David," she says, touching his cheek.

He starts to calm this time, and she can hear the squeakiness of his breathing as he gets more still.

"It's okay," she adds again.

"You're hurt," David mutters, moving his hand toward her neck, but he doesn't touch her there.

"I'm fine."

David looks over at the house. "What happened?"

"The Doctor hit you over the head," Allison tells him. "He was behind all of it."

"The Doctor? What do you mean?"

"Marcum Shale is the Doctor. He's the one who survived the fire."

David turns toward the open grave. His body as tall as the torches.

"Where is he?" David asks, still facing the place where he was buried for the second time in his life.

"Inside . . . I think I killed him."

David looks at her, his eyes cold as stone.

"I want to see," he says.

156

17

NINETY-THREE DAYS

Allison follows David inside. The stillness in the house has an edgy, uneasy quality. Something is about to happen, Allison thinks. Something bad.

It's darker than before. A few candles have burned themselves out, but the thickest one on the kitchen table still glows. David picks it up.

"Which way?" he whispers.

Allison points toward the hall. "It happened upstairs."

She stays close to him as they pass the photographs on the walls, and this time Allison lingers for a better look.

Black-and-white images cover the walls. Mostly of bodies. Dead bodies. Some with parts stitched together—like Frankenstein. Others with leather masks. One masked figure has been nailed to a cross. Two grayish monkeys have been crucified next to him. Another photograph shows a naked woman lying on a table. Her eyes closed. Her mouth gagged. Needles sticking out from the skin on her chest and arms and legs.

"David," Allison gasps.

He holds the candle up to the wall. The flame flickers near a photograph of a row of decapitated heads on spears, their lips sewn shut. A grimace tightens on David's face.

"Okay," he says, "this guy totally needs to get out more."

At the end of the hall they turn left toward the staircase. The landing above it appears empty now.

Allison rushes past David, climbing several steps. Pain hits her knees and ankles like an electric shock. Her body stiffens. She stops halfway up the stairs, grabbing on to the handrail and turning to David.

"The body is gone," she says. "He was right here."

Thick pools of blood cover the wood floor. She takes a few more steps, with David right behind her. Some loose plaster crunches under their feet. At the top she doesn't see any light coming from the office. The entire corridor is dark.

"Look," David says, holding the candle over the blood. Red footsteps lead down the hall. The left foot smeared more than the right.

"We have to get out of here," Allison whispers.

But David is already moving—mixing his own blood-stained footprints with the Doctor's. He hurries toward the far door and the light of the candle seems to disappear.

Allison follows quickly, running her fingers along the wall so as not to stumble in the dark.

"David?" she calls out.

A white light blinds her suddenly. A flashlight, she thinks for a second. But brighter. Much brighter . . .

Lampposts start glowing at twilight. Long rows of houses on both sides of the street. No cars along the curbs or in the driveways. No kids playing. Just houses—houses that Allison passes as she walks down the middle of the street.

She stops at one.

It's the Packers' house—the front door wide open. Welcoming.

It makes her smile, being home again. She listens for the sound of Brutus Packer Jr.'s drums, but everything here is quiet. She never realized how much the Packer house looks like all the other houses on the street. The same shingled rooftop. The same manicured lawn. The same trees scattered here and there.

At first the sound is barely noticeable. It's far away in the distance. A low, hungry rumbling. As it starts to get louder and louder, Allison can feel something beneath her feet. A shaking. The houses rattle. The trees rock back and forth. She glances at the Packer house again.

Suddenly the front door slams shut.

The rumbling is violent now. And loud. It almost knocks her over. She struggles to stay on her feet.

Then she sees it coming toward her—the cement street rolling like an enormous ocean wave. At its peak there is a fire like she's never seen. Bright red and orange. Molten. It devours the houses and the trees and the manicured lawns.

Destroying everything . . . everywhere.

It moves fast. Closer and closer.

Its fiery crest is about to break, to curl over and crash down onto her. It's about to reduce her body to ash.

She closes her eyes—

"You okay?" David asks, helping Allison to her feet.

She feels dizzy and off balance from the seizure, but she is far more shaken by her vision. Fire consuming the earth. The end of everything just like Jacob . . . just like the Doctor predicted.

"Yeah," she mutters, nodding. "Did you find him?"

He hesitates, glancing at the door at the end of the hall.

"What?" Allison asks. "What is it?"

"I found something . . . strange."

David takes Allison's hand and leads her to a small, empty room.

The window is uncovered and open. A cold wind pushes through, and for the first time tonight it feels good against her face.

"It's empty," Allison says, unsure about what David wants her to see.

"Behind you."

A full-length mirror leans against the opposite wall—unhung—and Allison sees her reflection in it. Slanted and distorted by the glass. Her body is bruised and bloody. Her hair messy. Above the mirror two numbers have been written in thick blood: 93.

"What do you think it means?" David asks, looking closely at Allison. The candlelight makes the gold in his eyes sparkle.

"He's gone," Allison says.

"Yes, but what does ninety-three mean?"

Allison pauses. "It's a countdown."

David helps Allison down the stairs, her body aching, her head still spinning from the seizure. Everything seems to hurt. In the living room a few candles still burn above the mantel, lighting the painting of nothingness.

David struggles with the dead bolt on the front door for a few seconds before it unlocks. Then he opens the door and ushers Allison through. She steps onto the cluttered porch. The boards creak under the weight of her body. The shadowy walnut tree spreads its arms over most of the lawn. But something is missing.

The rust-colored car.

It's gone.

She turns to David and notices that he is lingering in the doorway.

"Wait right here," he says. "There's something I gotta do."

"What?"

He goes back inside the house without answering.

"David," she calls out, stepping into the living room again.

She doesn't see him at first. She doesn't hear him either. *What's he doing?*

She moves farther into the room, and suddenly everything

brightens. The dark corners. The stacks of papers and boxes and books. A light pushes from the hallway. Crackling.

"David?"

The fire crawls forward. Flames start clinging to the walls, lapping at the pictures there. Pushing into the living room.

David hurries into the living room, a candle in his hand. He holds it to a stack of papers on the floor. They light as quick as the snapping of fingers. David moves down the line, from one pile to another. Each one catching fire and burning.

Soon the whole room is bright, the heat of the flames growing.

"Come on," David says.

They rush out the door and down the front steps. Allison almost falls, but David holds her up. He keeps her moving fast. Away from the house and the walnut tree. Down the rocky driveway. Back to her car.

Years ago, on the night before the fire, Allison didn't sleep. She kept tossing and turning and going over the plan in her head.

Well, it wasn't much of a plan. It was a thing that needed desperately to be done. There was no other way.

For weeks Allison and David and Jade and Ike and Emma had been trying to convince their parents to leave the Divine Path once and for all. But something was different about the adults after Jacob's final prophecy: "We are the Chosen who will rise up from the ashes to govern the new world with justice and wisdom, with vengeance and mercy. . . ."

After that Daddy couldn't stand to hear talk about leaving.

"But Jacob did this to me," Allison pleaded, pointing to the still-raw cut on her neck.

"Al, we're part of something real important here. And you don't just run away from the important things in your life. Even when it gets hard. You just don't."

No, Daddy never did get over what happened with Ma. He just kept putting his faith in Jacob, no matter what happened. Allison figured it had to do with Mel and making sure that bad folks were punished in the next life.

Daddy might have given up on life by the time Jacob strolled into town. But Allison wasn't going to.

So when she came up with a plan for killing Jacob, they all huddled close together on Allison's bunk and voted on it. Even Harold nodded with the rest of them. They all knew that Jacob was causing too much hurt. That he had to be stopped. Harold thought so too, but he didn't offer to help with the plan after that.

And no one asked. There are some things in the world that a person just can't live with. And Harold couldn't kill his father.

As they were talking it over, a noise came from outside. The loud snap of a branch. They all tensed—terrified that it was Jacob, that he was only moments away from bursting inside and sending them all to the Confessional for their treachery. But it must have been nothing. Everything got still again. They listened to the silence for a few minutes, then continued.

"Once Jacob is gone, we can get our parents back," Allison said before they all left her bed and climbed into their own bunks. It was what they wanted most of all. For things to be like they were before Jacob.

No one slept easy for the next three nights. They had to wait until Wednesday, when one of the adults went into town to refill the gasoline can.

The night it happened, no one slept. David and Jade went first. They grabbed the gas can by the only generator at camp. It powered the four lightbulbs of the main hall. The rest of the buildings didn't have electricity.

Ike and Allison waited by Jacob's cabin with the matches, while Emma kept a lookout—just in case someone made a late-night run to the crappers and saw them. It seemed like forever and a day before David and Jade showed up, Allison remembers. She could hear the gas sloshing in the can before she saw them rushing toward her in the dark.

Then they started pouring it along the base of each wall. Letting it soak in real deep. Jade also splashed some on the walls and the door so Jacob couldn't get out. There was no room for error.

Allison and Ike started at opposite sides of the building. It was dry out, and the matches flared up fast, even with the wind. But that was nothing compared with how fast the wood burned. It seemed like the entire cabin went up in a single blaze.

The shingles on the rooftop burned brighter than the rest, and wind seemed to make the fire angrier. More hungry.

Allison hadn't thought about what would happen next. She just assumed the rest of the Chosen would wake up and come running. They would try to save Jacob, frantically throwing water onto the fire. There would be screams and tears and prayers. But when the smoke cleared, it would be over.

No more cult.

No more Jacob.

They could finally go home.

But no one came running. The fire burned and crackled and roared. The dark sky became bright. And when the wind started carrying the flames from Jacob's cabin to the other buildings, Allison ran to wake up Daddy.

He and the other adults were sound asleep.

Perfectly still and quiet.

Allison whispered at first, then she started shaking him hard. She yelled. She even slapped his face.

Nothing.

Jade and David were doing the same to their parents, but no one moved.

Everyone—their parents, all of the adults—were dead.

Back at Jacob's cabin, as she stood in a circle with the only friends she had ever known, Allison looked around at the six of them, heads bowed as if they were too ashamed to look at one another.

Jacob must have poisoned Daddy and the others, she thought. Maybe when they passed around the chalice that evening during service. Or maybe it was something in the food.

With the fire raging and her daddy dead and Ike Dempsey gripping her hand so tight that she couldn't feel her fingertips, she couldn't think anymore.

The heat from the blaze started to make her back sweaty, and she leaned forward. There were sirens in the distance. Fire trucks and police cars. The fire must have been visible for miles, Allison figured.

The sirens got closer, but none of those sounds were louder than Jacob's last words to her:

"In five years' time," he said, "your greatest fear will consume you. It will rob you of your last breath."

Listening to the fire sizzle and gasp behind her, Allison wondered if he hadn't just been trying to scare them.

"What if it comes true?" she asked to break the silence, her voice hoarse and unsteady.

But no one looked up or said a word. They just held hands as the air around them filled with smoke and the white ash of burning flesh. . . .

A fire blazes behind them now. David drives her car, and Allison slumps in the passenger seat. Every muscle and bone in her body is dog tired. Sore. Her arms and neck still throb from the open wounds.

As the Doctor's burning house lights up the road and the trees all around them, Allison wonders why she doesn't feel more relieved. More safe at this moment. She and David survived. They're leaving Meridian for good, she thinks. But somehow she can't talk herself into feeling better.

She's always had an ear for words. When someone says something, she just can't get it out of her head. And right now she is replaying the Doctor's promise:

"Even if I let you walk out of here right now, there are still ninety-three days until the year's end. Ninety-three days for your greatest fear to find you. To consume you. It is his will."

Ninety-three days.

It's hard for her not to believe it now. Not after seeing Emma's eyes and the fire that devoured Ike and the way the wind blew dirt into David's grave. Not after having her own dream of the apocalypse. If all her other dreams have come true, then perhaps the Doctor is right. Perhaps there are only ninety-three days or less until she and the world die in fire.

"You know . . . I was just thinking," David begins, and Allison turns toward him.

"What?"

"This is the worst vacation I ever had."

Allison smiles. "Tell me about it."

"So . . . where do you want to go?"

"Anywhere but here."

"How about Philadelphia?"

"Philadelphia?"

"It's where my foster family is. I think you'll like it," David says, and she can tell that he really means it.

"You should meet the Packers, too," Allison adds. "They're a little crazy, but nice."

"Okay."

As the car speeds along, Allison tries to picture Philadelphia and the steps that Rocky ran up and down in that movie. She thinks that seems like a good place to imagine a better future— to hope for one, at least.

Right then David reaches for her hand on the leather seat and squeezes it. She squeezes back.

And for a second, just a split second, Allison thinks that the world might not end after all.